Just a Bit Ruthless

(Straight Guys Book 6)

Alessandra Hazard

Table of Contents

Part I

Chapter 1

The suit was conservative, gray, and boring.

Luke Whitford eyed his reflection in the mirror with a disappointed frown. He looked…fine, but the suit didn't achieve the effect he had hoped for: he didn't look older.

Maybe it had been too much to hope for.

Sighing, Luke ran a hand over his smooth jaw, wishing he had some manly scruff to hide his baby face. He was twenty-three, for God's sake. It was embarrassing that most people didn't believe he was of drinking age and he had to have his ID on him at all times.

Luke blamed his ridiculous mouth: because of his full upper lip his face seemed set in a perpetual pout. It made him look very young, and while normally it wasn't a problem, it was a pain in the ass to look like a sixteen-year-old when one had to attend an important business meeting. Not that he attended all that many important business meetings.

Luke smiled grimly at his reflection and squared his shoulders. Well, that was about to change. He was going to prove to his father that he could be trusted with the important stuff. Sure, his father was going to be furious when he found out, but this chance was too good to let it slip through his fingers. He wouldn't get a chance like this again. Normally back in England his dad kept him on a short leash, watching him like a hawk.

Luke would have liked to think that the reason for this was his dad's over-protectiveness, but he wasn't delusional: Richard Whitford simply didn't trust his son.

Luke tried not to take it too personally—Richard Whitford trusted no one—but it was time to change that. He hadn't graduated with honors from Oxford only to spend his life being a pretty face for his father's marketing campaigns. Luke had always hated it, but he was downright sick of it after the last two months he had spent in Moscow, attending meaningless events in his father's stead for the Russian branch of Whitford Industries.

The email Luke had received a few days ago was a welcome break from the mind-numbing routine he'd grown accustomed to. Well, technically, the message wasn't for him. If Luke hadn't been in Moscow, his father's people would have simply forwarded it to the main office in London where his father currently was. Strictly speaking, Luke was supposed to do the same instead of reading it, but he had been bored and restless and the message had intrigued him.

Richard,

My secretary seems to be having trouble getting through to you. She informs me she's been unable to reach you. I told her you were a busy man. But I'm a busy man, too. I'm also not a very patient man. We have things to discuss. Saint Petersburg, Feb 21st, 9 p.m., restaurant "Palkin." I expect you to be there. Don't be late. You know how much I hate tardiness. I would hate for our friendship to be ruined over such a small thing.

Roman Demidov

Luke had read the message several times. Something about it was off. The friendly tone seemed fake. Or was he just imagining that? He didn't think so.

Roman Demidov. The name sounded vaguely familiar, but Luke couldn't remember where he'd heard it. But the man, whoever he was, must be important enough to be able to assume such a superior tone with Richard Whitford. Hell, the guy was practically ordering his father around. Luke had never met anyone who had enough power—and nerve—to do that. Everyone knew Richard Whitford wasn't someone to be trifled with. Luke's father was known as the most ruthless, most powerful British billionaire—a billionaire who was rumored to have dealings with the Italian and Russian mafia. Luke wasn't deaf to the rumors about his father; they'd been around all his life, but no one could ever prove anything. Not even he, Richard's only son, knew for sure.

The fact that the email's sender wasn't at all worried about ramifications despite Richard's reputation meant that, whoever that man was, he wasn't someone to be trifled with, either.

He should have forwarded the message to his father when he had realized it. But Luke had always been curious—perhaps too curious for his own good.

It took only a few minutes of Googling to find the information Luke had needed.

Roman Danilovich Demidov, thirty-two, was a Russian oil tycoon and multi-billionaire. Apparently, he owned dozens of companies all over the world and sat on the board of dozens more.

A multi-billionaire by the age of thirty-two. That kind of thing didn't seem to be all that strange in Russia. Luke had noticed that many Russian tycoons were rather young.

But it wasn't Demidov's age that attracted his attention.

Luke was kind of embarrassed to admit it, but he couldn't help but stare at the photographs of the guy. Roman Demidov was a tall, dark-haired man with broad shoulders and the kind of muscle definition that most men could only dream of. He looked like a professional boxer rather than a successful businessman.

It was stupid to form an opinion of a man he'd never met, but the more Luke looked at Roman Demidov's pictures, the more disconcerted he felt. Even when the guy smiled, it never seemed to reach his eyes. That ice-blue stare completely dominated every picture he was in, drawing attention every single time. There was nothing attractive about those eyes. If anything, the cruelty lurking in them was downright ugly.

The guy was handsome enough, Luke supposed, if one liked cold, assertive men who looked like they could snap your neck and

be bored while doing it. Luke certainly didn't. But, for some reason, he had trouble dragging his gaze away. It was silly. It was just a photograph. A photograph shouldn't make him so unnerved.

Shaking his head, Luke checked the time on his phone. If he didn't leave the hotel soon, he was going to be late for his flight to Saint Petersburg.

Luke looked at the door leading to the adjoined room and sighed.

James. He should probably tell James that he was leaving Moscow. But then again, Luke wasn't sure his friend would even notice his absence. James was so depressed he didn't seem to care about anything these days.

Luke grimaced a little.

Seeing his friend in such a state almost made him start questioning his dream of finding love. Considering that love had turned James from a lovely, outgoing guy into a depressed, lovesick mess, love fucking sucked.

Luke's own experiences were pretty disappointing, too: all of his four boyfriends had turned from Prince Charming to royal dickheads. To be fair, he'd never felt anything remotely close to how love was described in trashy Harlequin romance novels (that Luke *wasn't* ashamed of reading) for any of his boyfriends.

He'd never felt the sort of love that made him giddy and breathless with it. To Luke's utter disappointment, what happened in romance novels was the complete opposite of what he experienced in real life. But then again, maybe he just had a special talent for falling into bed with jerks.

Smiling ruefully at himself, Luke headed for James's room.

Half an hour later, after managing to get James out of bed and extracting from him a promise to eat while he was gone, Luke was finally on his way to the Sheremetyevo airport.

Leaning back against the taxi seat, Luke stared out the window.

He felt kind of guilty for leaving James alone. He knew there was little he could do to help his friend, but it still didn't feel right to leave him while James clearly wasn't holding up well after the messy breakup with his fuck-buddy/best friend/pseudo-brother/soulmate.

Despite knowing James his entire life and being one of his closest friends, Luke knew he could never replace Ryan for James: those two had always been codependent as hell.

But Luke also knew he was one of the few people James trusted implicitly. They'd always had each other's back, had been there for each other when they first realized they were gay, and had even been each other's first kiss. James was the only person he'd told who he was going to meet.

Luke frowned as his thoughts returned to the upcoming meeting with Roman Demidov. Not for the first time, a sliver of doubt crept into his mind. He was flying blind here. He had no idea what the Russian tycoon wanted from his father. The results of his research on the guy weren't exactly reassuring, either. Roman Demidov had the reputation of a shark; it was said he controlled his business empire with an iron fist. Luke had searched Whitford Industries' database, but he didn't have enough clearance and couldn't find what connected his father to that man.

God, he was sick of being kept in the dark. Yes, maybe what he was doing was reckless, but it was the only way he could force his father's hand: if he learned something he wasn't supposed to, his father would have little choice but to trust him.

Maybe you aren't ready to be trusted.

The thought made Luke's stomach flip-flop. It was something he'd been trying to avoid thinking about. What was he going to do if the rumors were true and his father really had dealings with criminals? If his father was a criminal?

Would Luke *want* to be trusted with that sort of information?

"*My na meste,*" grunted out the driver as the cab stopped. "*S tebya dve tyschi rubley.*"

Luke flinched and looked out the window. He hadn't even noticed that they had already arrived at the airport.

"*Spasibo,*" he said, thanking the driver in his limited Russian and shoving fifty dollars into the man's hand. Luke had no idea whether it was enough or not: his Russian wasn't good enough to understand the driver's strange accent.

The driver shot him an odd look and muttered something under his breath—clearly something uncomplimentary.

Quite used to it, Luke grabbed his suitcase and got out of the car, hoping for a hassle-free flight to Saint Petersburg.

But of course, making an already stressful day worse, his flight was delayed because of the bad weather, and Luke barely had time to check in to the hotel he had booked in Saint Petersburg before hopping into another cab and giving the driver the address to the restaurant "Palkin." At least he'd had the foresight to wear a suit, so he didn't have to waste time changing clothes. It was a small comfort.

Luke sighed tiredly as he got out of the cab in front of the restaurant. At that moment, all he wanted was a hot shower and a date with the soft bed waiting for him back in the hotel.

Hoping he didn't look as tired as he felt, Luke straightened his shoulders and walked to the front entrance of the restaurant.

This meeting was important.

He couldn't screw it up.

The restaurant was well-decorated and elegant in an old-fashioned way. The attentive staff spoke excellent English, which was a relief. Luke handed his coat over and informed the polite hostess that he was there to meet Roman Demidov. The woman smiled before leading him to a table in the secluded corner of the restaurant.

Roman Demidov was already seated at the table, his body language relaxed, almost bored.

The pictures didn't do him justice, Luke thought. They failed to capture the intensity of his presence, and those eyes were actually more unsettling in person.

It took every bit of Luke's self-control not to blush and fidget as the man studied him coolly.

"Good evening. My father was unable to attend and sent me in his stead," Luke said, extending his hand for a handshake. "Luke Whitford."

Roman Demidov didn't move an inch, his pale blue eyes boring into him.

"Is this a joke?" he said at last, his accent non-existent. His low, cultured tone was impeccable by any standards. Even James's top-lofty, aristocratic father wouldn't find fault with it.

"Not at all," Luke said, taking the seat opposite him and trying not to let it show how nervous he was. "My father is currently in London. He's in the middle of important negotiations.

He can't leave on such a short notice, so he sent me in his stead."

The man remained as still and seemingly relaxed as he had been before. But Luke was pretty good at reading people. He didn't miss the slight narrowing of those blue eyes.

Roman brought his drink to his lips and sipped slowly, his eyes still trained on Luke. "I don't do business with children. You can't be older than sixteen, maybe seventeen."

Luke felt a blush color his cheeks. He'd known it would be an issue.

At times like this, he seriously considered plastic surgery to fix his ridiculous lips.

"I'm not a child," he ground out.

Before he could say anything to try to save this disastrous meeting from getting any worse, Roman pinned him with a look that could probably freeze lava. Luke couldn't *breathe*, caught in that gaze and unable to look away, his body tensing.

"If Whitford couldn't be bothered to show up, the least he could do was warn me so that I didn't waste my time." Roman stood up. "Go home, *malchik*."

And then he was gone, two silent bodyguards joining him on his way out.

At once, other sounds rushed in—soft piano music, hushed voices of other patrons—as if Luke had been in some sort of sound bubble, as if the sheer force of Roman Demidov's personality had muted everything else in his presence.

And then Luke realized what Roman had called him condescendingly: *malchik*. A little boy.

He glared at the vacated seat, a fresh flush of humiliation washing over him. He had the strong urge to get up and leave, but he fought it. He hadn't eaten anything since this morning.

He might as well eat.

Luke signaled the closest waiter.

The food was delicious, but he could barely taste it with the disappointment and humiliation still churning in his stomach. There was also a great deal of apprehension. Instead of forwarding the email to his father, as he probably should have, he had acted on his own and failed. Demidov had been pissed off by his father's no-show. The ramifications of that were…uncertain. Luke knew nothing about the man to predict his reactions.

He had no idea what the Russian wanted from his father, after all.

In hindsight, maybe he shouldn't have poked his nose where it clearly didn't belong, but he had been sick and tired of being kept in the dark and attending pointless events. He had just wanted to know what his father was up to. He had just wanted in. Maybe it had been stupid to go blind into this, but he had always been confident in his ability to fly by the seat of his pants—until that Russian tycoon with creepy eyes reduced him into a blushing, self-conscious *kid*.

It was snowing by the time he finished eating and left the restaurant.

Luke shivered slightly and hugged himself, once again thinking how inadequate his Burberry coat was for Russian winters. He'd never been so cold in his life.

Looking around and noticing a cab parked nearby, Luke smiled in relief and strode to it briskly, the snow crunching under his boots. For the first time that day, luck seemed to be on his side.

He got into the car, told the driver the hotel's address, and closed his eyes, his thoughts turning back to the disastrous meeting with Roman Demidov.

There was no point kicking himself. It wasn't his fault that the guy was a narrow-minded prick who thought it was beneath him to do business with someone who just happened to look very young. It was Demidov's mistake, not his. Luke was nowhere near as young and inexperienced as he looked.

But fucking hell, plastic surgery seemed increasingly tempting by the minute. One day, he was going to inherit his father's business empire, and he couldn't afford not to be taken seriously only because he looked like a pouting teenager.

It also probably didn't help that he had curly, dark gold hair that could be tamed only by either shaving it off or slicking it back with gel. And since his vanity didn't allow him to shave his unruly hair off, Luke was resorted to growing it out a little and slicking it back. On the rare occasions he let his curls run free, his friends ribbed him mercilessly that he looked like an angel.

Luke pulled a face at the thought. When he had been younger, he hoped his looks would mature and roughen with age, but by now he had pretty much given up on that hope: he still hadn't lost the baby-like smoothness of his skin, or the delicate, cherubic curve of his cheek, and his height remained disappointingly average. Coupled with his dimples and plump lips, it was no wonder he had trouble being taken seriously by his father's associates.

No, Luke didn't have low self-esteem. He knew he looked good. He had no problem attracting men when he wanted to get laid.

But he was also a walking magnet for all sorts of perverted creeps. Looking sixteen when one was twenty-three just invited trouble.

He wasn't even surprised anymore when guys asked to see his ID before having sex with him. It was actually a good sign if they did.

Luke was pulled out of his gloomy thoughts when the car started accelerating.

He opened his eyes. "Hey, you sure it's safe…" His words trailed off as he looked out the window. Wherever they were, they weren't in the center of the city. How long had he been daydreaming? "Mate, I'm pretty sure the hotel isn't in this part of the city."

There was no reaction from the driver. Maybe he didn't speak English?

"*Eto nepravilnaya doroga*," Luke said slowly in Russian, hoping his pronunciation was okay.

The man said nothing. The car kept accelerating. It didn't even seem like they were in the city anymore.

His heart pounding, Luke bit his lip. Surely it wasn't what it looked like, but it was better safe than sorry, right? Slowly, he slipped his hand into the right pocket of his coat, where he kept his phone. Cold sweat appeared on his forehead when his hand found nothing.

His breathing elevated as he searched his other pockets.

Nothing.

Fuck. Fuck, fucking fuck.

Luke forced himself to stop panicking and think. He met the driver's eyes in the mirror.

"Look, you don't want to do it," he said, trying to keep his voice calm and authoritative. "My father isn't someone you want to piss off."

"*Zatknis*," the driver barked out. [Shut up.]

There was also the unmistakable sound of the safety being taken off a gun.

Luke took a deep breath. There was no point panicking. Panicking was worthless and stupid. Think, Luke.

He looked back. It was dark outside, but he could see two black SUVs following them. So the driver wasn't working alone. It wasn't an ordinary robbing. They knew who he was.

Luke wished he was more surprised, but he wasn't. He was the son of a billionaire. His father had many enemies.

"Whatever they're paying you, I'll pay you five times that much," he said.

The driver laughed shortly. "Dead men don't need money, *anglichanin*," he said in heavily-accented English.

A shiver ran up Luke's spine at the implications of the guy's words. His stomach sank. The driver was too scared of the person who had hired him to betray them, no matter what Luke offered him. Fear was a powerful motivation.

Which basically meant Luke was screwed.

Now he could only hope that, whoever was behind this, they just wanted a ransom. And nothing more. Nothing worse.

Chapter 2

Time dragged by. Minutes, hours, Luke couldn't tell. His tired mind kept conjuring up one horrible scenario after another as he waited for them to get to their destination, wherever it was. The driver had told him to shut up when Luke had tried to interrogate him, so he was left alone with his thoughts.

As a teenager, Luke thought he had his life all figured out. He was going to fall in love with a nice, insanely attractive guy by the age of twenty who would adore him back, he would be in a steady, committed relationship with him for a few years before marrying him, they'd get lots of kids, and he'd live his happily ever after. Thinking about it made him smile now. He was already twenty-three, the man of his dreams had failed to materialize, and now he might not live to see the next day.

Yeah, life was funny that way.

It seemed that at some point he dozed off, because the next thing Luke knew, he was startled awake when two pairs of hands dragged him out of the car. The muzzle of a gun pressed into his lower back. "Walk," someone barked out.

Dazed and disoriented from sleep, Luke did as he was told, blinking at his surroundings. They seemed to be in the middle of nowhere. It was still dark, but he could make out the looming woods a few hundred feet away. The woods surrounded the house he was being half-dragged, half-pushed toward. The snow was very deep, almost up to his knees, heavy and wet, and Luke struggled to move his feet.

"Faster, *blyad*," said the same thug, pushing him.

Luke held back the sharp retort on the tip of his tongue and tried to walk faster. Resisting was useless at this point. Angering his captors was just plain stupid. There were eight of them, and all of them seemed armed. He had to cooperate—for the time being.

At last, they reached the house and he was roughly shoved inside. Luke fell to his hands and knees, gasping. The thugs laughed, exchanging some jokes at his expense.

Ignoring them stoically, Luke got to his feet and looked around. The hall wasn't at all what he had expected. It was tastefully and elegantly decorated, practically screaming of money.

The sound of the door opening caught Luke's attention. A tall, beefy man with Slavic features and cropped blond hair walked out of the room. The thugs immediately stood at attention, dropping their leers and sneers. The blond exchanged a few words with one of the thugs, too fast for Luke to understand them. The thug addressed the blond as Vlad.

At last, Vlad turned his gaze to Luke.

Luke met his eyes, refusing to show fear. One of the few lessons his father had drilled into him was that one should never show fear in the face of adversity.

"What do you want?" Luke said calmly. "Why did you kidnap me?"

Vlad looked him over. "I don't have to explain anything to you, English," he said, his accent very heavy. His eyes lingered on Luke's mouth for a touch too long before he glanced at the thug he'd been talking to and gave him a short order in Russian.

If Luke understood correctly, he was to be locked upstairs in the gray room and was to be fed once a day until further orders.

Luke's stomach dropped at hearing that. He had hoped he would get at least an explanation.

"Please, could you tell me anything?" Luke tried again. "Why am I here? Do you want money?"

Vlad's eyes flicked to his mouth again, making Luke's blood run cold.

At last, the blond shook his head. "I have orders not to talk to you," he said and looked back at his men. "*Zaprite malchishku v seroi komnate.*"

Two thugs grabbed Luke and half-shoved, half-dragged him upstairs. Luke didn't fight them and he didn't try to speak to Vlad again. The Russian wasn't the one giving orders. He wasn't the one behind Luke's kidnapping. Vlad might appear powerful, but he was a mere pawn. He wasn't the one Luke should be negotiating with.

If Richard Whitford had taught his only son anything, it was that in any unfavorable situation, there was always room for negotiations. Any situation could be turned to his advantage—or at least could be swayed a little in his favor. But one didn't negotiate with pawns. One negotiated with the king. Luke was looking forward to meeting him.

Chapter 3

A slice of stale bread. A small bottle of water. That was his daily ration.

By the end of the week, the last remnants of Luke's optimism were extinguished by the hunger gnawing at his insides. He felt fatigued and weak, almost dizzy at times. In all his life he had never known true hunger, not until now. His stomach contracted in painful spasms and all he could think about was food. He needed glucose-rich food. Luke knew if he didn't have low blood sugar, it probably would have been nowhere near as bad, but it was a small comfort when hunger kept him awake at night, curling up on the narrow bed, the only piece of furniture in the room.

The worst part was how some of the guards liked to torture him by eating all kinds of delicious-smelling food in front of him, laughing when Luke stared at it with hungry eyes. Sometimes, if the guards were drunk or bored, or both, they used him as a punching bag, but even that was preferable to the sight and smell of food he couldn't eat.

Their employer hadn't made an appearance. From what Luke had overheard, he wasn't even in the house. Now Luke felt silly for expecting a visit from the main bad guy.

It wasn't a cheesy Hollywood movie where the villain always came to gloat and share his evil plans with the victim. In all likelihood, Luke and his well-being were completely insignificant in the grand scheme of things to the person behind all of this.

This kidnapping clearly was nothing personal, and the bad guy didn't have to explain anything to him. The thought smarted. He'd never felt so powerless in his life.

Luke was curled up in bed, shivering from cold and holding his stomach, when he heard the sound of the locks turning. He tensed. They had already fed him that morning. Were the guards bored again? His ribs still hurt from the last time they had been bored.

Luke tried to stand, but it probably wasn't a good idea considering how fatigued he was, so he settled for sitting up and leaning against the headboard. Even that drained him of what little energy he had left, and he had to breathe deeply to fight the sudden bout of dizziness that washed over him. He wasn't going to faint, dammit. Not now.

The door opened and closed, but his vision was still swimming and he could only make out the blurry tall figure that had entered the room.

Finally, his vision sharpened, the world came into focus, and Luke found himself gasping as he met the cold blue eyes of Roman Demidov.

Fuck.

In the past week, he had thought of Demidov a few times, wondering if he had anything to do with the kidnapping, but he had dismissed the idea. Roman was a condescending prick, and his eyes totally creeped Luke out, but it didn't necessarily mean the guy was a criminal. He had told himself "filthy-rich Russian tycoons" didn't equal

"Russian mafia." Well, clearly he'd been wrong in this case.

For a long moment, there was only silence as they looked at each other.

Luke fidgeted, feeling more than a little self-conscious. He probably looked pathetic. His curls were no longer tamed by gel, his fringe falling over his eyes. Luke was wearing the same blue dress shirt from a week ago, but now it was crumpled, dirty, and stained with blood. At least he had been allowed a shower yesterday (only because the thug that brought him food had complained to Vlad that he stunk).

All in all, if Roman Demidov had been unimpressed with him a week ago, when Luke had looked his best, he was unlikely to take him seriously now that he looked like a beaten-up, half-starved kid.

"What do you want with me?" Luke said calmly—or at least he tried to, but his voice was weak, the words shaping up oddly in his mouth.

Roman's inscrutable expression didn't change.

He continued looking at him in silence, his gaze sharp. It was a hundred times more unnerving than any words.

Luke fought the urge to squirm. "Look, whatever issue you have with my father, I know nothing of it. Just let me go, okay?"

The man stepped closer and grabbed his chin in an iron-like grip, so hard it hurt. "What are you playing at?"

Luke blinked up at him, confused. "I don't understand," he said slowly, trying not to wince from pain or show his fear.

Roman's lips thinned.

"Who do you take me for?" he said. "Why did Whitford send to me his only son? Unarmed, no bodyguards, no precautions at all? Kidnapping you was laughably easy."

Luke couldn't help but laugh, though his lips were still swollen from the last beating he'd received, and it hurt a little. "Sorry? You sound disappointed."

The man stared down at him, as if Luke were some strange creature that didn't make any sense. "You can't possibly be such a clueless child," he said in disgust, letting go of him and straightening up.

Luke studied him curiously, the beginnings of a plan forming in his mind. If the guy was unable to see past his boyish looks, he could use that. Maybe his youthful appearance would finally be good for something. He could play it up, pretend to be totally harmless and clueless — pretend to be the vulnerable teenager he certainly wasn't. Luke was an optimist at heart. He was a firm believer that completely evil people didn't exist. Even the most heartless, hardened criminals would think twice before mistreating a vulnerable kid. Wouldn't they?

Well, it was worth a try.

Luke put on his best puppy-dog eyes and looked up at the other man from under his eyelashes, letting his exhaustion and fatigue show on his face. "I'm starving," he said softly. "If you don't want me to get sick, you should feed me better. I have low blood sugar. I feel sick and dizzy if I don't get to eat properly."

There was no flicker of remorse on Demidov's face. "You're alive," he said curtly. "That's the only thing I care about. A weakened captive is less of a hassle."

Nice.

Refusing to give up, Luke bit his lip and dropped his gaze. "Okay."

Silence.

He waited with bated breath, but with every passing second it was becoming increasingly obvious that this man was as cruel and unfeeling as he looked.

"You didn't answer my question," Demidov said, laying his large hand on top of Luke's head gently.

Luke went motionless, not daring to look, not daring to breathe. There was something about that gentleness that unsettled him to his core. He knew very little about this man, but one thing he knew for certain: he didn't have a gentle bone in his body.

"I d-don't know what you expect me to say," he managed, fighting the wave of dizziness brought by fear. He stared down at his bare toes. "I know nothing about my father's dealings with you. He tells me nothing. He didn't know I went to meet you. I had no idea what I was getting into when I decided to go in his stead."

The long fingers carded through his curls ever so gently.

Luke couldn't breathe.

The fingers tightened before yanking his head up by his hair. Hard blue eyes bored into his. "Do you expect me to believe this?"

"You're hurting me," Luke said, letting tears well up in his eyes. He managed to make his bottom lip tremble. "I'll tell you everything I know, I swear."

The painful grip on his curls didn't lessen one bit, but Demidov's gaze flicked down to Luke's wobbling lip. The look lasted a fraction of a second, but Luke didn't miss it.

Oh.

He dropped his gaze again as a new thought occurred to him. Luke truly hadn't intended to go this route—a part of him couldn't even believe he was seriously considering it—but...But. He wasn't a damsel in distress. He refused to be a damsel in distress and timidly wait to be rescued. It was his own fault that he had acted recklessly and gotten himself in this predicament. Not to mention that his father was going to skin him alive if he had to pay some outrageous money to ransom him. Yes, Luke had screwed up, but it was still his chance to prove to his father that he could handle tricky situations by himself. If he could manipulate this powerful man, he would more than prove to his father that he wasn't useless, that he was smart enough and resourceful enough, that he could be trusted.

But could he do it if a mere look from this man made his knees weak with fear? If a pseudo-gentle touch made his heart pound?

Luke lifted his gaze to the other man again. His stomach tied in knots when his eyes locked with Roman's. The Russian wasn't unattractive. Far from it. He was ruggedly handsome, with his short, dark hair, straight nose, and his square jaw dusted with dark stubble. His name suited him: he reminded Luke of the warriors of Ancient Rome. He was very fit, his shoulders wide and powerful under the black turtleneck he was wearing, his arms and chest thick with muscle. If the guy wasn't so tall, he would have looked beefy. As it was, he just looked like a perfect killing machine. There was a quiet, carefully restrained aggression in his body language, something lethal and dangerous. Although Luke was of perfectly average height and build, he felt small next to this man. Breakable.

Luke moistened his lips with his tongue.

The painful grip in his hair tightened, yet Roman's voice was very soft. "I want answers. Now."

Luke took in a deep breath, trying to shake off his nerves.

Roman Demidov was just a man. Just a man like him or James. All right, maybe not like him or James, but still. Every man, no matter how hardened and clever, was susceptible to a bit of manipulation and persuasion. He just had to find the right approach.

"I'm telling the truth," Luke said quietly, keeping his tone open and naive. "I got the email by mistake. I went to meet you without telling my dad because I wanted to prove to him that I was mature enough to be involved in the family business."

Roman snorted derisively.

Swallowing the biting remark that came to mind, Luke said, "You don't take me seriously. Why do you think my father is any different?"

Bingo. He could see that Demidov was finally inclined to believe him.

The tight grip in his hair loosened, turning into a gentle caress again. Luke wasn't sure which was actually worse.

"So you're here only because you're a stupid, reckless child," Roman said, his tone mild.

Inwardly, Luke imagined punching him in the nose with great relish and in great detail. Outwardly, he caught his lip between his teeth and shrugged. "Could you tell me why you kidnapped me?" he asked, trying to ignore the fingers still buried in his hair.

"No," Demidov said.

"Aren't you afraid you'll be the prime suspect in my kidnapping?" Luke said, cocking his head. "There's the email. There are people who know I went to meet you." Well, James had seen a photograph of Roman and could likely give his description to the police.

Demidov didn't look worried in the least. "We had a very public meeting at a very public place, a meeting arranged through official channels." His voice remained soft, his unnerving, empty eyes fixed on Luke's curly hair as his fingers ran through it gently. "There are numerous witnesses who saw me leave well before you and get on the flight to Sochi, where I spent the week. The president of Russia himself can confirm my alibi."

Luke's eyebrows flew up. Who, exactly, was this man? How could such a relatively young man achieve such power?

Three guesses how, Luke thought, suppressing a shiver. "So are you demanding a ransom from my father?"

Roman gave no response.

"What did my father do to anger you so much?"

No response.

Luke gritted his teeth before remembering himself— remembering his plan. He couldn't show his anger. He couldn't throw temper tantrums. He had to be good. He had to somehow soften the guy up.

He had to seduce him if necessary.

Luke felt his cheeks color a little. The task seemed daunting, even impossible. This man couldn't have gotten to where he was by being susceptible to manipulation. He was dangerous. If he even suspected what Luke was up to…

His stomach twisted into knots.

"At least tell your people to bring me food, please? I feel sick." Luke looked up at Roman and wet his lips with the tip of his tongue. "I'm so hungry."

Roman's gaze followed the movement of his tongue. If Luke didn't feel so shitty, he would have laughed. It looked like Neville, his first boyfriend, had told him the truth for once. The asshole had lied to him for months, hiding that he was married, and when the truth had gotten out—when his wife had turned up at Luke's flat—Neville actually had the nerve to blame Luke for steering him off the "right path," claiming that no red-blooded straight man could look at his lips and resist thinking of sticking his cock between them. At the time, Luke had felt so stupid, pathetic, and *dirty*, but maybe, just maybe, Neville had been right. Maybe.

Luke breathed carefully, painfully aware of Roman's fingers in his hair, of those cold eyes scrutinizing him. It was impossible to tell what was on the guy's mind. Although Luke had caught Roman's gaze lingering on his mouth, his gaydar remained silent.

Everything in him screamed to be careful with this man, that a head-on attempt at seduction and manipulation wouldn't be well-received. He had to keep in mind that the guy, despite his impeccable English, was Russian. While being gay was still far from easy back home, things were much worse in Russia.

Although Luke didn't like to generalize and stereotype, he couldn't help noticing that anti-gay rhetoric seemed to be ingrained in Russian culture. Every other swear word used by his guards was a homophobic slur, whether it was relevant or not. Luke had never been called a faggot—*pidaras*—as often as he had been this week, even though he gave the guards no reason to think he was gay.

Luke guessed he must be thankful that their homophobic views prevented them from doing anything that would make them faggots, too, but it wasn't very comforting. He felt ill at ease surrounded by such hostility and disgust toward what he was. If they found out he really was gay, Luke had a sneaking suspicion that it would be a green light for the guards to use him as they pleased: they would rationalize that he was just "asking for it"—and of course using a dirty faggot wouldn't make them gay.

That was why he had to tread carefully with this man. One wrong move would invite a disaster.

"Please," Luke said softly. "I'll be completely cooperative. I'll do anything you want." He kept his voice free of innuendo, making sure his expression was earnest. He couldn't initiate anything—that would be blatantly obvious. His gut told him Roman Demidov belonged to the category of men who got off on power and who liked to see submission, but not necessarily sexual submission. Luke could fake submission. If he could play his cards right, he mightn't even need to sleep with the guy.

The thought of actually having sex with this man, having Roman's hands on his body while those disconcerting eyes looked down at him, sent a shiver through Luke's body.

Against his will, his gaze was drawn down to the other man's muscular thighs. He could see the outline of Roman's cock beneath the fabric. Although it wasn't hard, it looked massive, long and thick. Swallowing, Luke licked his dry lips, a squirmy sensation in his stomach. Fuck, a cock like that would completely wreck him—and a man like Roman Demidov was unlikely to be gentle.

He would be rough, commanding, and caring only about his own pleasure. Luke could practically see it: the Russian's heavy body on top of him, crushing him as he moved between Luke's thighs, using Luke as a hole for his dick—

Roman released his hair and stepped away. His eyes were narrowed as he studied Luke's face like a hawk.

Luke held his gaze, hoping that he wasn't blushing and his dirty thoughts weren't written all over his face. Sometimes he hated his vivid imagination. He wasn't sure why he had been thinking about that. In all likelihood, Roman wasn't attracted to him in the least and he had nothing to fear. He had more pressing things to worry about than the guy's cock—like getting some food into his empty stomach.

"Please," Luke said quietly.

Some emotion flickered across Roman's face. He stared at Luke some more, his expression inscrutable once again, before turning around and leaving.

Luke sagged back, disappointment nearly crushing him. He'd failed. Again.

Then, he heard Roman's cold voice, muffled by the door but clear enough:

"Daite malchishke chto-nibud poyest suschestvennogo. Myortvym mne on ne nuzhen." [Give the boy some decent food. He won't be of use to me dead.]

A slow, little smile curled Luke's lips.

It might be a small win, but he felt his optimism returning.

Baby steps.

Chapter 4

Roman Demidov strode away from the captive's room, his mood darker than ever.

The maid he met on the way to his office took one look at him, paled, and ducked her head, as if hoping he wouldn't notice her. Smart little thing. Too bad he was too worked up right now.

He grabbed her arm. She froze, barely breezing.

"Lena, isn't it?" he said quietly, eyeing her blond hair and slim figure. She wasn't particularly pretty, but she had plush, soft-looking lips. His eyes lingered on them. His jaw tightened.

"Yes," she said meekly, glancing up at him for a moment before dropping her gaze. He could see her pulse beating madly at the delicate base of her neck. She was scared of him. Or perhaps she was excited. Probably both.

Silently, he opened the door to his office and went in. He knew she would follow him inside.

He wasn't wrong. He rarely was.

"Close the door," he said.

The door clicked shut behind him.

There was a moment of silence, broken only by the howling of the wind outside and a tree branch banging on glass. The room was very warm despite the freezing weather.

There was no heating in the gray room, Roman thought, recalling the boy's shivering body. The lack of heat was a strategic decision: usually the "guests" staying in the gray room were to be weakened by hunger and cold. Certainly not to be pampered and fed properly.

Roman's jaw clenched.

"You may leave now," he said. "Or you may undress."

After a brief pause, there was the sound of clothes rustling.

He took a deep breath, trying to relax his shoulders. It wouldn't do to hurt the girl. He rather liked her—when he didn't feel like breaking something. Or someone.

"Over my desk," he murmured.

He wasn't in the mood for elaborate foreplay. Not today.

She was wet when he pushed into her.

She let out soft moans as he fucked her, fully clothed but for his open fly, his fingers gripping her hips in a punishing grip, his teeth gritted and his eyes staring into the snowstorm raging outside.

He barely felt himself coming. It was just a release, an outlet for his dark mood. It did nothing toward easing it.

"Thanks, love," he said afterward, pulling a few bills out of his pocket and placing them on the desk by the girl's panting form.

She smiled dazedly, grabbed the money and her clothes, and hurried out of the room.

Roman tied the condom and threw it into the rubbish bin.

Dropping himself in his chair, he lit a cigarette and closed his eyes.

Blyad. Goddammit.

Even despite the fuck, the boy's golden curls and plush, cherry pink mouth stood before his eyes. That mouth. It was a cross between an angel's mouth and a whore's.

He wanted to fucking wreck it.

He'd wanted it from the moment he first saw the boy in the restaurant, all dressed up and trying to play grown-up games without knowing any of the rules.

Roman wasn't used to denying himself what he wanted. He always got what he wanted. Except he couldn't fuck the boy's mouth, couldn't split those lips on his cock and choke him on it as his body wanted.

For fuck's sake.

He wasn't a faggot.

No matter how pretty that mouth was, his physical attraction to a *boy* didn't sit well with him. He didn't like what he couldn't understand or control. It was also inconvenient as hell. He ought to be thinking about the best use he could get out of Whitford's only son and heir. Instead, he had spent minutes petting the boy's soft curls and staring at his mouth. Unacceptable. And it was completely unacceptable that he had relented and ordered the guards to feed the captive better only because the boy batted his eyelashes and asked him prettily.

Roman sneered, disgusted and irritated with himself. He should have starved the kid. He should have starved him until those pretty lips became pale and chapped, until those rosy cheeks hollowed out from malnutrition, until the boy turned ugly and pathetic.

How an ordinary, bull-faced man like Richard Whitford had managed to produce a son who looked like that was a goddamn mystery.

Roman threw his cigarette into the ashtray and pressed a button on the intercom. "Bring me a bottle of vodka, Vlad."

He could sense Vlad's surprise even without seeing him. "But you don't drink," Vlad said slowly. "You never drink."

Roman murmured, "You've always had a penchant for stating the obvious, Vlad." His voice hardened. "Get me that bottle now."

"Give me a minute," Vlad said, probably realizing Roman was in no mood to tolerate his insolence this time.

Vlad had been his head of security for almost ten years. He was very loyal—he was one of the few people Roman trusted implicitly—but Vlad tended to forget himself, expressing his disagreement with Roman's actions in situations most people would never dare to.

The door opened and closed.

Vlad walked in and placed a bottle of vodka on the desk, his pale brows drawn together. He opened his mouth but shut it upon meeting Roman's gaze.

Roman stared at the bottle in front of him. His mouth was dry and the urge to drink was definitely still there, but he squashed it easily enough. He hadn't touched alcohol in fifteen years and he had no intention to do so ever again. He was still in control of himself and his life. He was still in control.

One boy with cocksucking lips wasn't going to change that.

"Take it away," he said, satisfied.

Vlad didn't comment, just took the bottle back. His gray eyes observed him in silence.

"What?" Roman said without any inflection.

"What are you going to do with Whitford's brat?"

Roman lit another cigarette and took a long drag. "Haven't decided yet. I didn't exactly plan this." The boy had practically fallen into his lap.

Vlad cocked his head to the side, his expression curious. "It's very unlike you to act impulsively."

Roman shrugged with one shoulder. "I know a good opportunity when I see one."

Vlad nodded slowly. "So does that mean you'll use the boy?"

Use the boy.

"Of course I will use the boy," Roman said, looking at the bottle still grasped in Vlad's hand. He dragged his eyes away. "Whitford needs to be taught a lesson."

"And pay what he owes you," Vlad said.

"It's not even about the money," Roman said, eyeing the cigarette in his hand. "The Englishman played me." He thought of Michail's lifeless eyes and crushed the cigarette in his hand. "No one gets away with that."

"Don't you think it's cruel to drag the kid into it?"

"He's twenty-three years old," Roman said flatly. He had checked. Twice.

Vlad snorted. "It's hard to believe, isn't it? If I didn't know better, I wouldn't give him a day over sixteen. He looks so…innocent, I guess."

Roman shot him a sharp look. "Why the sudden interest?"

Vlad shrugged.

Was he avoiding Roman's gaze?

"He's interesting. In the past week he never cried once, didn't go into hysterics even when he was brought in. He's practically a perfect captive."

Roman continued studying him, watching Vlad grow uncomfortable under his scrutiny.

"Is that so?" Roman said.

"Yes."

"He has bruises on his face," Roman said, watching his head of security. "And from the way he was breathing, his ribs are at least bruised. I gave no such order."

Vlad swallowed.

Roman didn't soften his expression, watching Vlad squirm. It wasn't that he gave a fuck when his men roughed up his "guests" a little. But he didn't tolerate it when his orders weren't carried out precisely. He hadn't given his men permission to touch his newest acquisition.

"You know how the lads get when they're bored," Vlad said, still not quite meeting his eyes.

"I know," Roman said. "But it's your job to rein them in."

Vlad nodded, his wide shoulders slumping. "It won't happen again," he said, turning to leave.

"Did you participate, too?" Roman said.

Vlad froze.

"I thought so," Roman said, very softly.

"Look—" Vlad started, his ears red. "It happened only once. I know I shouldn't have done it, shouldn't have let it happen, but it was fucking freezing outside and I had a few sips of vodka to warm me up—I know it's no excuse—"

"It really isn't."

"I know!" Vlad said, frustration and regret lacing his voice.

"It's just—there's something about that kid that makes all my men agitated, and I'm not an exception."

Roman's eyes narrowed. He had an inkling what had his men so agitated. It wasn't even the boy's pretty face or blowjob lips. It was the air of innocence about him. The urge to dirty him up would be nearly irresistible to men who didn't have a shred of innocence left.

On one hand, it was a relief to know he wasn't the only one affected by the boy, but on the other…it was clear that leaving Luke Whitford in the care of his men may not be a good idea if they were so easily influenced by the captive to the point of forgetting their orders. It was dangerous. Roman surrounded himself with only the best men, but he was aware few had his self-control. Some inebriated idiot might be too susceptible to the boy's pretty lips and doe eyes.

"Are you saying you can't control your men?" Roman said in a low-pitched voice.

Vlad gulped. "I'm saying I can't control them around the kid," he replied with a grimace. "No matter what I threaten them with, when they get bored or drunk, they want to have fun. And the boy looks…" Vlad licked his lip. "No homo, but he looks fucking beautiful all beaten up and bruised."

Roman's fingers twitched. "Is that so?" He stared at the fire cracking in the fireplace. That boy was dangerous. If he could get even his normally unflappable head of security so agitated…

"Roman Danilovich?" Vlad said tentatively.

He looked up. "I'm disappointed in you, Vlad."

His jaw tightening, Vlad nodded briskly, his beefy body tense and wary.

Roman went silent for a while. He always enjoyed this part. Let him stew for a bit.

"I expect that such…a lapse of judgment will never happen again," he said at last.

Vlad relaxed, breathing out. "It won't. I promise."

"Not good enough," Roman said. "Whitford's son will be moved to the room adjoining mine."

Vlad's eyes widened. "What—it's a security risk—"

"You know what's a security risk, Vlad?" Roman said cuttingly. "When my head of security gets too fucking *distracted* at work."

Vlad flinched. "I promise it won't—"

"Your promises are not enough. I'm not punishing you only because you have proved in the past that I can trust you with my life. But now you proved I can't trust you or your men with Whitford's brat." Roman pursed his lips. "Get the room secure and have the boy moved into it. From now on, until you prove to me I can trust you with this, I will be the only one who has contact with the boy. Dismissed."

Vlad nodded and left with a chastised look on his face.

As soon as the door shut after him, Roman leaned back in his chair and breathed out, unclenching his fist.

Goddammit.

This was the last thing he needed.

Chapter 5

His head throbbing with a headache, Roman was in a foul mood when he entered his room later that night. He'd lost a great opportunity to increase his profit in Central Europe just because he hadn't been there in person to see the deal through. Couldn't they do anything without his hand-holding?

Sighing, he went to the en-suite and got some Tylenol from the first aid kit. Swallowing the pills, he stiffened at the noise in the adjoining room.

Of course—the boy. He'd almost forgotten about his order to move him there.

Roman unlocked the door, pushed it open, and entered the room.

Luke Whitford was sitting on the bed, rubbing his stomach. He looked up, his eyes widening when he saw Roman. Otherwise, he didn't even flinch. Vlad had been right about one thing: the boy wasn't prone to useless hysterics.

"Thank you," Luke said. "For the food. They fed me before bringing me here." He sank his teeth into his lip, hesitation flickering in his eyes. "Why am I here? Your people didn't bother to explain."

Roman walked over. "What makes you think I will?" The thought was amusing.

The boy cocked his head to the side, looking up at him almost shyly, his thick dark eyelashes framing his deep brown eyes. "Nothing," he said, chewing on his lip. "But I'd like to know. Please."

So polite. Too polite.

Roman's lips thinned. He laid his hand on Luke's head and tugged on the golden curls. "Do you take me for a fool?" he said, knowing his grip must be painful. Tears of pain welled in the boy's eyes.

"I-I don't understand," Luke whispered.

Roman glared at those wobbling lips. "Do you really think a few soft-spoken words are enough to manipulate me?"

The boy dropped his eyes, guilt and disappointment flashing through his face. "I'm not very good at it, am I?" he said with a wince and a crooked smile.

"No," Roman said. The boy had been too well-behaved and innocent for that to be real.

Luke hugged himself, looking up at him warily. "Are you going to punish me for trying to manipulate you?" His voice cracked a little.

Roman stared at him, considering his options. He could always order his men to rough him up, but the idea didn't sit well with him. He blamed Luke's deceptively youthful looks.

Roman would readily admit he wasn't a good man. He'd done things that had surely reserved him a place in hell...if an afterlife existed.

But he'd done those things to adults, not children.

Luke Whitford wasn't a child.

But the air of innocence he had about him coupled with his baby face fucked with Roman's mind. No, he didn't want to hand the boy over to his men. But the boy must be punished. If Roman didn't punish him, Luke might start getting ideas. Roman had been too soft with him as it was.

He said, "You will kneel in that corner, clasp your hands behind your back and remain that way until seven in the morning. No breaks, no bathroom, no sleep."

Luke looked like he wanted to protest, but he closed his mouth and silently went to the corner and knelt on the floor, facing the wall. As far as punishments went, it was far from the worst, but Roman knew how uncomfortable and painful it would be to keep that position.

"It goes without saying that this room is under constant video surveillance," Roman added, staring at the mop of curly hair. "You will not like your punishment if you choose to defy me. Is that understood?"

"Yes, sir," the boy murmured.

Sir.

Roman left the room, trying to ignore the way that little English word pleased something in him. An honorific like that didn't exist in Russian—or rather, they were old-fashioned and no longer used.

He had to admit that sometimes the English language might be superior to his mother tongue.

Chapter 6

The first hour was okay. His stomach was full, the room was warm, and he even had something like a plan.

Luke was relieved and a bit surprised by the punishment Roman had chosen for him. He had expected worse. He had been a little apprehensive when he devised the plan to get caught in the act, but it all went seamlessly. Roman had bought it. Now that the guy was assured of his own superiority and cleverness, assured that he could see right through Luke, it would be easier to soften him up and lull him into a false sense of security. Luke felt a pang of shame before reminding himself not to be silly. Roman Demidov was a criminal. Men like him deserved nothing less. Besides, it wasn't like he was planning to kill the guy or something. He just wanted to save himself. He just wanted to go home. That was all.

The second hour was harder, and the third hour was worse. He was getting more uncomfortable by the minute. His knees were sore from kneeling on the floor for so long and his arms and shoulders were starting to ache.

The fourth hour made it clear why Roman had chosen such a seemingly soft punishment.

Luke's entire body ached from the stiff position he was forced to maintain, his feet were asleep, and his neck and back hurt pretty badly. Luke had to remind himself that this was the plan. He had to be "punished" and accept his punishment for the Russian to think he was beaten into submission—so to speak.

But he almost gave up by the end of the fifth hour.

His eyelids kept closing, his bladder was full, he was exhausted, his bruised ribs still aching from the beating he had received a few days ago, and he wanted to sleep so much it was a physical effort not to.

The clock on the wall seemed to be mocking him by marking time ever so slowly. Minutes dragged. Time crawled by at such a snail's pace that he wondered whether the clock had stopped working. Luke kept himself awake only by imagining creative ways to torture and kill Roman. The asshole was probably sleeping like a baby right now in a soft, comfy bed, not a care in the world. Luke couldn't feel his limbs anymore.

By six in the morning, he became vaguely aware that his face was wet from tears running down his cheeks. *Everything* hurt, and he just wanted to curl into himself and finally pass out.

He realized that he was no longer alone only when a pair of strong hands pulled him up by the shoulders. Luke's legs gave out. He couldn't move, his feet still asleep and his entire body hurting. He cried, hiding his wet face in the man's wide shoulder.

"Shh," said a gentle, low voice, long fingers stroking his hair. "You did well."

A part of Luke's dizzy, sleep-deprived brain screamed at him to stop clinging like a baby to the asshole who'd done this to him, but it felt very distant and unimportant. This felt good—the hands felt good—and he was so, so tired.

Sniffling into Roman's shoulder, he let the man lift him and carry him to the bathroom. Once there, Roman put him down by the toilet, letting Luke sag back against him, undid the fly of Luke's trousers, and said, "You can relieve yourself now."

Any other day, Luke would have told him to fuck off. But he was exhausted, sleep-deprived, and hurting all over. Maybe he should have felt mortified by his physical and emotional helplessness, but he was past the point of being embarrassed.

"If I step away, you will fall on your ass." Roman's voice was dry, with a hint of impatience.

He probably would.

Silently, Luke pulled his cock out with his numb, clumsy fingers. He honestly tried to do as he was told, but with Roman's wide chest pressed against his back and his hands on Luke's hips, he just couldn't relax enough to do it. It also didn't help that his bladder was so full—it was so full it was difficult to piss.

"I can't," Luke whispered, close to tears again. He was so, so tired. He wanted...God, he just wanted to close his eyes and be taken care of.

"You can and you will," Roman said. "I won't have you soiling your clothes and stinking my rooms."

His rooms?

But before he could ask, Roman knocked his hand off, grabbed Luke's cock and said, "Just relax and do it. I have more important things to do than change your nappies."

Luke stared dazedly at their reflection in the mirror. He looked like a fragile doll in Roman's arms. Roman's hand was around his cock. Roman's other hand moved up to his belly and started rubbing it in circles. There was something vaguely disturbing about the man's touch: it was so matter-of-fact, as if…as if Luke was just a thing that belonged to him.

And yet, somehow, it helped. Luke almost moaned in relief as his reluctant bladder finally obeyed.

It was a completely surreal experience when Roman shook his cock a little before tucking it back in. Once again, Luke's exhausted mind noted how business-like and freakishly proprietary Roman's touch was, as if doing this was completely normal, as if Luke was a thing belonging to him and that he was doing maintenance on. It should have made him angry, but anger required energy, and he had none. His body was running on fumes, days of starvation making it weak and the lack of sleep making his processing speed much slower.

"Now bed," Roman said, lifting him again with one arm and easily carrying him back into the bedroom. He dropped Luke on the mattress and said, "Your clothes stink."

Luke blinked up at him blearily. "Of course they stink," he mumbled. "Your goons didn't let me wash them. I have nothing else."

Roman's lips pressed together. Between one blink and another, he was gone.

Luke's eyelids had already closed when he was shaken awake. He protested, turning onto his stomach and hugging his soft, perfect pillow.

"You will sleep after you change," a familiar, hated

voice said. "You stink."

"Uh huh," Luke mumbled into his pillow.

He heard some swearing in Russian, but his mind was half-asleep and couldn't translate it.

"*Blya, eto mne chto li nado,*" Roman said, his tone irritated, before he pulled Luke up into a sitting position and undressed him quickly. Luke didn't open his eyes, only vaguely aware of being forced into something long and soft. It smelled good.

He was all but shoved face down on the bed, but then a gentle hand stroked his hair. "Sleep."

"Uh huh," Luke muttered before hugging his pillow and falling into a deep, untroubled sleep.

Chapter 7

When Luke woke up, it was well into the afternoon, although if it wasn't for the clock on the wall, there would be no way of knowing. It was snowing outside the window.

Luke rubbed at his eyes and stretched in the soft bed, feeling deliciously well-rested and comfy. His muscles ached a little, but he felt more comfortable than he had in ages. He still wasn't sure why he had been moved from his old room to this suspiciously nice one, but he hoped it wasn't just a fluke.

Then, he recalled something. Had Roman really told him these were his personal rooms?

Luke flushed, remembering the circumstances of it. Fuck. Had he really let that man manhandle him, hold his dick while he pissed, and generally treat him like a thing? His thing?

Luke's stomach did a little flip-flop. Suddenly, he had a nearly irresistible urge to run. Run somewhere far away from that strange man with cruel eyes and gentle, proprietary hands.

Though…he couldn't deny that it all had gone rather smoothly.

Better than Luke could have hoped.

Yes, he had been punished, and it had sucked, and his little clingy breakdown afterward was cringe-worthy, but Roman had been almost nice to him. The guy had taken care of him when he didn't have to. He could have left Luke lying there, exhausted and helpless, until he pissed himself and fell asleep on the hard floor. He had even changed Luke's clothes and put him in bed. Granted, Roman had been hardly gentle as he did so, but still. Luke decided to count that as a small victory. He always liked to be optimistic.

Yawning, Luke stretched and sat up. His muscles felt a little sore but nowhere near as bad as he had feared. His eyes fell on the nightstand and widened. There was a big tray with food there. With all sorts of food. There were even fruits and vegetables.

Luke grinned, his stomach growling.

Nope, shower first, Stomach.

His mood much improved, he padded into the bathroom, glanced at the mirror and went still, noticing what he was wearing. A long-sleeved, white shirt. It clearly belonged to someone taller and wider in the shoulders than him: it came down almost to his knees. Was it Roman's?

A shiver ran up his spine at the thought. Normally he wouldn't have cared—he would've just been happy to get out of his dirty clothes—but after last night's surreal experience, wearing the man's clothes made him distinctly unsettled. Not to mention that he was naked under the shirt.

There was another door leading from the bathroom. Luke stepped to it and listened. Nothing.

He pushed the door, but it didn't budge. Locked. Of course. Even if he really was in Roman's own rooms, as

Roman had implied, he would hardly be left alone, free to wander around as he pleased.

Sighing, Luke started undressing. He needed a shower. He needed to relax and stop thinking about last night.

But as he stood under the stream of warm water, Luke's thoughts kept returning to it. Something about it bothered him a great deal.

It wasn't like Luke was clueless about disciplinary punishments and everything they entailed: contrary to his appearance, he wasn't an innocent, inexperienced boy. Far from it. He was actually pretty familiar with that kind of lifestyle thanks to his second boyfriend, Alan, who was into BDSM and had convinced him to try it. In the end, after they experimented a little, Luke had told Alan that, while he respected his lifestyle, he didn't like being whipped, chained, and flogged.

Alan hadn't exactly been happy to hear that, and Luke still winced every time he thought of their ugly breakup.

But the thing was…He and Alan had done it by the book—they had used safewords and everything, they had trusted each other enough—but it just didn't work. It didn't do anything for Luke. While he had liked some of the stuff they had done—like being held down and fucked roughly—mostly he had found "punishments" annoying and silly rather than arousing, and he had never really felt impressed by them or particularly submissive. So the whole thing with Alan had convinced Luke that stuff like that did nothing for him.

Until this morning.

He wasn't sure how appropriate it was to compare last night's experience to his experiments with Alan.

He and Roman certainly hadn't been playing. There had been no safewords involved. It had been a real punishment—punishment that had reduced him to genuine tears—and the experience hadn't been sexual at all. Yet it shook him to the core.

Luke knew BDSM didn't always involve sex or even whips and chains; sometimes it was a little more complicated than that.

The truth was, last night's punishment and what happened afterward had felt far more intense and intimate than the kinky sadomasochistic sex he'd engaged in with Alan. Luke's memory of last night was pretty disjointed for obvious reasons, but the feeling of utter vulnerability, of being powerless, was clear and sharp even now.

And it made him uncomfortable as fuck—because for a few minutes, it had felt *good*. It had felt good to cry in Roman's arms and seek comfort from him, which was just...just fucked up. He didn't trust the guy at all. How could it feel good? Was he touched in the head?

Frowning, Luke turned the shower off. Uneasy to remain naked longer than necessary, he briskly toweled his body dry and slipped back into Roman's shirt, for the lack of any other options. His clothes were nowhere to be seen.

He stared in the mirror again, doubts clouding his mind.

Whatever happened last night—or rather, this morning—couldn't be allowed to happen again. He was ready to play the role of a vulnerable good boy to lull his captor into a false sense of security, but *play* was the key word. Only an utter fool would make himself truly powerless and vulnerable with a man like Roman Demidov.

* * *

Luke wasn't sure what had woken him up. He became aware that he was lying on his side, the sheets tangled at his feet. Something told him not to open his eyes, so he didn't. He listened, straining his ears, unsure and anxious, goosebumps running down his arms.

It was still night: he could hear an owl hooting in the distance, an eerie sound that made the hair on the back of his neck stand up. But there was something else. Someone else.

There. The barely audible sound of breathing.

Keeping his own breathing calm and even, Luke opened an eye slightly. He had left the bedside lamp on when he'd gone to sleep, so he had no trouble seeing his surroundings. Except whoever was in the room with him — and he *knew* who it was — stood on the other side of the bed and Luke's back was turned to him.

Then, he became aware of something else. His shirt had ridden up, leaving his ass and legs completely exposed to Roman's eyes. Luke's first urge was to yank the shirt down, but if he did that, it would betray he wasn't asleep. Luke didn't feel like he was ready to face this man after their last disconcerting encounter.

His exposed skin prickled, the tension in his body growing. Why wasn't Roman *doing* anything? Why wasn't he leaving? Why had he come at all in the middle of the night? Luke had fretted and waited all evening, expecting Roman or someone else to come, but no one had.

Thankfully, he'd been left with enough food so hunger wasn't a concern. In the end, for lack of anything better to do, he had gone to sleep, figuring a businessman of Roman Demidov's caliber would have more important things to do than visit a clueless rich kid who was useful only as a bargaining chip.

Except Roman was here now. Luke was sure he wasn't imagining the subtle scent of his cologne mixed with the faint smell of cigarettes. His muscles quivered with adrenaline, his heart beating so fast he felt dizzy for a moment. Why wasn't Roman moving? What was he looking at? What was he thinking about? And why the hell did Luke care?

"You're as terrible at pretending to be asleep as you are at manipulating."

Luke stiffened.

Chapter 8

The figure on the bed seemed to stop breathing, going rigid at the sound of his voice.

Roman's brows furrowed. The boy was scared of him. While it was neither unexpected nor entirely unwelcome, it would only complicate things. He couldn't have Luke fearing him too much. This time he needed…a gentler approach if he was to accomplish what he had decided to do after seeing Luke's reaction to the punishment. The way the boy had clung to him, seeking comfort and trusting him enough to fall into exhausted sleep in Roman's presence…it had opened new possibilities.

There were certainly far easier, faster, and less convoluted ways to make Richard Whitford pay, but this one would crush Whitford if implemented right. If Roman could condition Whitford's only son, make the boy completely dependent on him, then he would have the keys to what Whitford treasured the most: Whitford Industries, his pride and joy. Roman wasn't too concerned that Whitford didn't trust his son. If the boy had no clue about business, all the better.

Hold your fucking horses, Roman told himself. As the proverb went, he mustn't put the cart before the horse. He had to gain Luke's affections first for the plan to work. That wasn't going to be easy, even taking into account Luke's submissive inclinations.

The truth was, Roman had misgivings about the plan. He didn't like what he couldn't control.

And he couldn't quite control his own reactions that morning. When he had found himself with an armful of shaking, needy boy, it hadn't been a conscious decision to comfort him. It was all instinct. Luke's submissiveness had messed with his head, making him react instinctively—as any good Dom would react to a sub's physical and emotional needs after a scene. The problem was, the punishment he had given Luke was never meant to be anything but punishment. The boy's needy body language afterward shouldn't have triggered his instincts.

But it did.

Roman was no stranger to power play. He derived a certain pleasure from power games in everyday life; sometimes, if the mood was right, his body itched for it, too. Most people considered him a cruel man, and they weren't wrong.

But he wasn't a cruel lover, never had been. Granted, he wasn't a gentle lover, either. He liked it rough, liked the rush of power he got when he reduced someone into a pliant, submissive mess—it was far more arousing than rape and the unnecessary cruelty some of his people indulged in—but he took good care of his sex partners. Sexual gratification wasn't always the point when he was in the mood to play, but normally an attractive woman's genuine submission made him want to fuck her.

Roman had never thought a male could affect him the same way, yet this young man with his obscenely pretty lips and natural submissiveness did, and Roman had found himself wanting to do wicked things to him for hours before tucking him in.

He hadn't, of course. He still had some self-control left.

But now it was being tested again.

Luke was still barely breathing. Roman's eyes moved away from the mop of curls to the boy's tense neck, down his back clad in Roman's own shirt, to the perky, perfect little ass and shapely, toned legs.

Gritting his teeth, Roman tore his gaze away and rounded the bed.

The boy's eyes were wide open, his cherry pink lips parted slightly. Luke licked them. "Why are you here?" he said, finally tugging the hem of Roman's shirt down.

Roman's eyes tracked the movement. He sat down on the bed, inches away from Luke's head.

The boy visibly stiffened, watching him warily. In the yellow light of the lamp his hair looked like a golden halo.

"This is my house," Roman said. "Everything in this house is mine. You're not a guest here. I can come and go as I please. I don't have to explain myself to you. I can do whatever I want." *I can do whatever I want to you.*

They stared at each other in silence, tension stretching out like a taut wire between them.

An owl hooted outside the window.

Luke swallowed. "I know what you want," he whispered. "I'm not stupid."

Roman threaded his fingers through the golden locks. So soft and pretty. "And what do I want?" he said.

Seconds passed, loaded with tension.

At last, Luke said, looking him in the eye, his cheeks tinged with pink, "You want to fuck my mouth. You keep looking at it."

It was a struggle to keep his face impassive.

"I'm not a faggot," Roman said, without any inflection.

He wasn't a raging homophobe, at least compared to his men, but he certainly wasn't a sympathizer. He'd never understood why some men would prefer flat chests, hairy asses, and unattractive legs to women's soft, shapely bodies.

Luke smiled crookedly, flashing a hint of a dimple. "My ex wasn't a faggot, either. Didn't stop him from putting his prick in my mouth. What guy doesn't like getting his prick wet? A faggot's mouth is just as good as any woman's."

So the boy was gay, as he had suspected. And Roman could see that despite his light tone, Luke's casual smile was put on, forced. It was clearly a sensitive subject to him, and yet…there was something else there.

Roman studied him for several moments. The boy was blushing a little, his pupils dilated and his breathing unsteady. He kept licking his lips.

Interesting.

"You almost sound like you're trying to convince me to do it," Roman said.

A nervous laugh left Luke's lips. "You scare me shitless. Why would I want to have my throat stuffed with your cock?"

Roman's blood rushed downward. "You have a very vivid imagination."

Luke's eyes went wide and his pretty pink blush darkened to crimson.

They stared at each other for what felt like an eternity.

Unhurriedly, Roman unzipped his trousers with his free hand and pulled himself out.

Luke dropped his gaze and stared at Roman's half-hard cock inches away from his face. "What?" he whispered hoarsely.

Carding his fingers through the boy's curls, Roman said, "Isn't this what you want?"

Luke shook his head, his eyes fixated on Roman's hardening cock.

"I think it is," Roman said, nudging the head of his cock against the boy's madly beating pulse before dragging it up Luke's neck to his cherry lips. So fucking pretty. Luke was breathing unsteadily, his eyes wide, cheeks flushed. Roman watched him avidly, keeping his face cool and collected, as if his erection wasn't brushing Luke's lips, as if he didn't want to shove his cock down the boy's throat and fuck it raw.

"Suck," Roman said quietly.

Luke swallowed and shook his head again, but it didn't look very convincing, considering the fact that he had an erection, too. One glance was enough to confirm it.

"I'm not going to force you," Roman said. "Ask me nicely and I'll give you a cock to suck."

"No," Luke said, squeezing his eyes shut. He looked pained and tense as Roman nudged his cock against his lips. Luke whined when Roman slapped his mouth with his cock.

"No," the boy said again, even as he mouthed Roman's cock greedily. "Please, don't do this."

Ah. A heady wave of arousal washed over Roman.

If this was what Luke was into, *fine*.

"Red, yellow, green," Roman said, gripping the curls tighter in his hand.

Luke blinked up at him in confusion. Shit, he seemed completely out of it already. Finally, understanding dawned in those dark eyes.

"Green," Luke murmured, surprise flashing across his expressive face—no doubt he was surprised that the asshole who had kidnapped him was decent enough to give him safewords. The boy couldn't know that Roman was playing a long game. He would be nice enough to Luke. He would be so good to him that soon the boy wouldn't be able to *breathe* without him.

"Suck it, *blyad*," Roman said, letting his voice become harsher.

"No," Luke said, shaking his head, his eyes dark and hungry.

Roman slapped him across his cheek. Luke whimpered and looked up at him, panting. Roman yanked the boy's face onto his hard cock and hissed as Luke's wet mouth engulfed him, plump lips cradling his aching erection.

Fucking hell.

Before he could stop himself, before he could think twice about what he was doing, his hips were snapping forward, his cock thrusting in and out of the boy's mouth with obscene, wet sounds.

Luke was whimpering quietly around the length fucking his throat, his eyes squeezed shut, tears glistening at the corners of them.

Roman couldn't look away.

Watching his thick cock fucking such an angelic, innocent face seemed beyond filthy and wrong. Despite the tears in his eyes as Roman's cock choked him, the boy was hard, his slim fingers working furiously on his own erection. An angel and a whore.

"Such a cockslut," Roman said softly, hands cradling and stroking the boy's cherubic face as his hips snapped forward and back. "How many cocks did you suck, you little faggot?"

Luke moaned around his cock. Apparently he liked being forced, used, and called derogatory names. Appearances could certainly be deceiving, though Roman wasn't one to judge. People got off on the weirdest shit, him included, and it meant nothing.

This meant nothing.

So he let go, taking his pleasure in Whitford's son's mouth and telling him what a slut he was, telling him that he was born to have a cock in his every hole, all the while cradling and stroking Luke's face as if he were made from something precious. The boy reacted beautifully, sucking his cock like a goddamn pro and leaning into his hands, seeking his touch. He didn't resist when Roman rolled him onto his back and, straddling his chest, fed his cock back into Luke's waiting mouth. After that it was a blur of fucking, the boy's hoarse moans and his own grunts as he thrust into the wet perfect heat of that mouth.

At last, he came, swearing through his gritted teeth, and watched the boy swallow his come with eagerness that shouldn't have been so damn arousing.

"Mmm," Luke said, panting, when Roman pulled out. He looked fucking wrecked, his lips even redder and fuller than usual, his dark eyes glazed over.

Roman let his softening cock drag across the boy's flushed cheek before flopping onto his back next to him.

The room was silent but for the sound of their ragged breaths.

Roman tucked his cock in, zipped up, and looked back at the boy.

He still lay sprawled on the mattress, the expression on his face dazed, smooth legs splayed out, his hand wrapped loosely around his spent cock.

Roman resisted the urge to get out of the bed and leave without a word, to get away from this room and everything that had happened in it. He wouldn't, of course. Doing so would be a demonstration of weakness, would betray how much the sex had rattled him. He wasn't rattled. Just annoyed with himself. He wasn't supposed to have sex with Luke Whitford, at least not at this point. Using him as a hole for his dick was unlikely to make the boy trust him, considering what Luke had implied about his ex.

He had needlessly complicated everything, adding something unpredictable, something that could either hinder or help his plans. It could go either way.

Luke turned toward him, his eyes still glossy and soft. "You gave me a safeword."

"It might come as a surprise to you," Roman said, his voice very dry, "but I don't actually enjoy raping people." He let the corner of his mouth curl up. "Unless they're into it."

A faint blush appeared on Luke's cheeks. He pursed his lips. He looked like a disgruntled kitten. "I'm not into it," he said haltingly. "You forced me."

Roman raised his eyebrows. "That's not how I remember it."

"I'm not sick," Luke said, looking even more disgruntled. "Only sick, twisted people are into that kind of thing."

Roman pulled a cigarette and a lighter out of his shirt pocket. "Is that what nice people teach their kids these days?" he said, lighting the cigarette. "What a load of bullshit." He inhaled deeply and blew a cloud of smoke at the ceiling. "Newsflash, *kotyonok*: what gets you off says nothing about your character. I know a man who gets off on being pissed on by women. He's one of the most assertive, confident men I've ever met."

There was an uncertain, confused look on Luke's face now. He opened his mouth and closed it several times, but in the end, he settled on, "Don't call me *kotyonok*. I know what that means."

Roman snorted. "I called you a faggot, cockslut and *blyad*, and you didn't mind, but now you're bothered that I called you a kitten." Kitten was apt. The boy did look like a disgruntled kitten.

Luke pursed his ridiculous lips. "I hate it when people use endearments they don't mean."

"I'll keep that in mind, *solnyshko*," Roman said. He almost laughed at the face the boy pulled.

"Sunshine isn't any better than kitten," Luke grumbled, glaring at him uncertainly.

"You know Russian pretty well," Roman said, a little surprised by the fact. The boy's father didn't know two Russian words.

"I'm pretty good at understanding it, but I'm horrible at speaking it."

Luke shot him a probing look. "I don't get it. You're being almost nice. You're not a nice person."

"What makes you think so?" Roman said, deeply amused. Actually, he couldn't remember the last time he had been so amused. "Because I had you kidnapped and locked up here?"

Luke shook his head, looking distinctly uncomfortable.

"Because I'm an evil Russian oligarch?"

Another shake of head.

Roman propped himself up on an elbow, regarding the boy curiously. "No?"

Luke bit his lip before saying, "You have cruel eyes."

"Cruel eyes," Roman repeated, a sardonic smile curling his lips. "And here I was being so nice and giving you a cock to suck on."

Luke flushed. "I didn't ask for your cock."

"You all but begged me to use your mouth, kitten. I was being a nice host."

"Nice. Right."

"That's right," Roman said, brushing his knuckles over Luke's silky-soft cheek. The boy shivered but didn't shake the hand off. Roman smiled. "But I've changed my mind. I gave you what you wanted. Time to pay up."

"Pay up?" Luke said, his expression turning wary. Smart boy.

"Yes." Roman let his knuckles trail down the boy's neck, thinking of a suitable demand—one that would advance his plans. Ideally, it would be something that would make the boy get used to him, maybe even get attached to him. It couldn't be anything sexual. Luke would come to him asking for his cock.

Until then, Roman would keep his cock out of the boy's mouth, no matter how pretty it was.

His eyes dropped to that pursed lush mouth and lingered.

He wanted to taste it.

The sudden desire was so strong it threw him off. Using the boy's mouth as a hole for his cock was one thing. Wanting to kiss it was another. Roman couldn't actually remember the last time he had wanted to kiss anyone. He didn't really do kissing.

"You know, you make me very nervous when you get that look on your face," Luke said with an uncomfortable chuckle.

"What look?"

"Like you're contemplating murder."

"Not at the moment," Roman said, stroking the boy's pulse with his thumb. "Kiss me."

"What?" Luke squawked.

"Kiss me."

"Why?" Luke said, glancing between Roman's eyes and lips.

"Because I said so," Roman said, irritation lacing his words. He couldn't remember the last time his orders were questioned so much.

"Right," Luke said after a moment. "But I don't want to."

"You sucked my cock and enjoyed it," Roman said, leaning down to him. "Open your mouth."

Luke glared at him, his breathing uneven and his body still.

Roman looked down at his lips and licked his own.

The boy's mouth was positively sinful.

Both lips were plump, cherry pink and enticing, the upper lip fuller than the bottom one.

On any other male face that pouty mouth would have looked ridiculously out of place, but not on this one. Roman's own mouth practically itched to taste, bite, and suck.

So he did.

He didn't try to be gentle. He wasn't a gentle man. He took Luke's chin in his hand and kissed him, rough and greedy. The boy tasted like Roman's come, but instead of disgusting him, it turned Roman on and he kissed him deeper, harder, hungrier, his fingers tightening on Luke's jaw. Luke moaned quietly, starting to squirm against him, his plump lips clinging to Roman's—

Roman pulled away.

Breathing harshly, they stared at each other, Luke's eyes wide and dark, his lips swollen from Roman's cock and teeth. Fuck. It took all his strength not to nail the boy to the mattress then and there.

"I told you you'd enjoy it," Roman said, and he was surprised by how normal his voice sounded.

A storm of different emotions flickered through Luke's expressive face. "If you can turn me on, it doesn't mean I like you."

"I don't need you to like me, love," Roman said, getting out of bed and straightening his clothes. He leaned down to brush his lips against the boy's well-used mouth, relishing the way Luke tensed and shivered. Roman bit Luke's lip lightly. "Liking me isn't a requirement. You can keep on hating me."

You'll need me, anyway.

He left, without bothering to see Luke's reaction.

Once he was back in his own room, Roman came to a halt and took a deep breath. Pressing a button on the intercom, he said tersely, "Send me a woman. Young. Blonde. Average height. She must like it rough."

If Vlad was surprised to receive such a request at three in the morning, he didn't say anything. "Yes, Roman Danilovich. You'll have her in half an hour."

He did.

And if he thought about the boy in the next room as he slammed into the woman, he was the only witness and judge.

Chapter 9

Roman was up to something; Luke was sure of it. He was playing some game, the purpose of which wasn't entirely clear to Luke yet.

He hadn't known what to expect from the other man after last night. Heck, he hadn't known what to expect from himself after last night. He wasn't sure how to act around Roman anymore. His half-baked plan to pretend to be a clueless, vulnerable kid to make Roman drop his guard around him seemed so laughable now.

He didn't need to pretend. He felt terribly self-conscious and vulnerable after revealing to Roman Demidov, of all people, his most embarrassing kink: that he got off on being forced, used, demeaned and called derogatory words. None of his former boyfriends had known about that particular kink. Luke had always been too ashamed to tell them, feeling like a freak for getting off on something like that. He didn't understand what was wrong with him: he *hated* homophobic slurs and felt sick at the mere thought of actually being raped, so why did he turn into a different person when he was turned on? Why couldn't he be normal?

"I don't want to talk about it," Luke said, keeping his eyes firmly on the tray of food and resisting the urge to move away from the man next to him.

The bed seemed so small with Roman's long, wide-shouldered body stretched out casually on it. Did he have to sit on Luke's bed? There was a perfectly good chair in the room.

"Why?" Roman said.

"I don't know about you, but sex is kind of a private matter for me," Luke said as calmly as he could, cutting a piece off an apple with his knife and sticking it in his mouth. He would wonder why Roman allowed him to have a knife if he had any delusions about his ability to take him on in a physical fight. It was obvious Roman's muscles weren't the result of workouts and diet. Roman moved with the fluidity and confidence of a man who knew how to use his body as a weapon.

The question was: Why was this dangerous—and likely very busy—man wasting his time watching Luke eat and asking about things Luke had no desire to discuss?

It was all very bewildering, especially after last night—after Roman fucked his mouth, kissed him until his toes literally curled, and then went to his bedroom to fuck some woman whose moans Luke could hear even through the two doors separating their rooms.

Luke pursed his lips.

"You weren't such a prudish little thing last night," Roman said.

"Last night was a mistake," Luke said stiffly, looking at the leftovers on his plate and fighting a blush. "I'm not— I'm not like that."

"Like what? Gay?"

"No, obviously I'm gay." Luke lifted his eyes to Roman. He tried not to look at the little wisps of dark hair peeking out from under Roman's halfway unbuttoned shirt. "Look, you got the wrong impression. I'm not into that kind of thing—not really. I've had four boyfriends and I didn't do anything like that with any of them."

A faint smile curled Roman's lips. "I'm flattered."

When Luke glared at him, Roman's smile widened, becoming amused. The smile actually touched his cold eyes, and, for the first time, Luke realized how attractive and charming this man could be if he wanted to. The thought unsettled him. He didn't want to notice it.

"It doesn't say much about your relationships if you couldn't tell your partners what you were into," Roman said, studying him through his hooded eyes.

Sweeping his gaze around the room, Luke said, "It's not—it really isn't a big deal. A relationship is more important to me than some weird kinks." Luke tucked a stray curl behind his ear. "It's not like I'm that into it. I'm not a freak."

Roman's assessing stare was starting to get on his nerves.

"What?" Luke said uncomfortably.

"Your parents divorced when you were eight," Roman said.

Luke blinked at the abrupt change of topic. "Yeah," he said, unsure where this was going or why Roman suddenly wanted to talk about his parents' divorce, of all things.

"My sources say you were the main point of contention. Your mother wanted custody, but your father won it. He restricted your mother's access to you."

Roman's face was impassive as he recited the bare

facts of one of the most difficult periods in Luke's life.

Biting the inside of his cheek, Luke nodded.

Roman continued, "The details of the divorce were difficult to find, but apparently your father claimed that your mother was a bad influence and wasn't fit to raise you. Why?"

Luke picked up a banana and started to peel it. He knew he didn't have to answer. He didn't talk about this even with his friends. But then again, Roman wasn't a friend. Luke was unlikely to ever see him again after this whole ordeal was over. Who would it hurt to answer truthfully? He couldn't see how Roman could use this information against him. Maybe if Roman saw that he had nothing to hide, it would help Luke in the long run. Not to mention that at this point Luke was ready to talk about anything other than his embarrassing kinks.

"My father didn't like how close she and I were," he said with a shrug. He took a bite of the banana and chewed slowly. "Mum and I were best friends. She kind of…she was—is—an amazing mother, but she always wanted a daughter and had little clue how to raise a boy. All she had was me, and she did her best, but Dad was always away and very busy, so…"

Luke shrugged again, eyeing the banana in his hand. "One day he came home and found me playing a grown-up in my mother's clothes. He got angry." The understatement of the century. He still flinched whenever he remembered the brutal flogging he'd received that day. Luke cleared his throat. "He accused Mum of turning his son into—into a f-freak." He cleared his throat again. "The funniest thing is, I'm not even into cross-dressing. I was just playing, as all kids do."

And okay, he still did like colorful and pretty things, but that was neither here nor there.

Luke put the banana down and took a sip of his coffee. "Anyway, my parents divorced, and my father hired a male tutor to make me…manly. To 'make a man out of me' and get rid of all the freakish nonsense Mum put in my head."

He chuckled, looking into his cup.

He supposed it all had worked out in the end. His mother was happily married now, living in Los Angeles with a husband who loved her and three beautiful daughters she could spoil rotten without fearing her husband's wrath. Luke loved his half-sisters, although he only got to see them a few times a year and had little in common with them.

"A freak," Roman said in a strange tone. "I wouldn't call you 'manly.' Do you think it makes you a freak?"

His fingers trembling a little, Luke put his cup on the tray and looked at Roman. "If I like sucking cock and taking it up the ass, it doesn't make me unmanly."

He was proud of how firm and sure his voice sounded. He felt anything but, his chest tight with a familiar panicky feeling. He felt eight all over again, trying to defend himself from his father's derisive, cutting words. *I'm normal, I'm normal, I'm normal.*

No, he wasn't normal. He'd always known that, hadn't he? His father had used to comment derisively about his "effeminacy" until Luke had learned to hide it better. Hell, even James, who was gay himself and his closest friend, used to tease him, albeit good-naturedly, for being too romantic and girly, so Luke tended to tone his personality down even around his friends.

He dressed conservatively and had learned how to sound pragmatic and practical, had learned it so well that it became second nature to him.

But no matter how hard he tried, he couldn't completely erase the part of him that wanted to be *pretty* and looked longingly at patterned, colorful shirts—shirts that would make him look camp and effeminate and would make him a target for his father's scathing criticism.

"No, what you like in bed has nothing to do with who you are," Roman said, watching him carefully. "But you're implying there's something wrong with not being 'manly' enough. You don't sound like someone completely comfortable with who you are."

Averting his gaze, Luke let out a small laugh. "I'm gay, and I'm proud of it."

Roman put his thumb under Luke's chin and tipped it up, bringing their faces close. "Are you?" he said quietly. "Is that why you're still in the closet? Or why you hide your curls and dress like a boring, middle-aged businessman? When I first saw you, I saw a little boy who seemed to be forcing himself to be something he wasn't."

Luke could only look at him, his throat dry and thick. "I'm in the closet because I don't have the most progressive dad in the world and because my dad happens to be a dangerous man with a quick temper. I dress that way because I want to look older and be taken seriously by assholes like you." It wasn't a lie, but why did it feel like he wasn't being completely honest? Luke glared, his fingers shaking. "It's not because I suffer from internalized homophobia or something like that. Not all gay men are stereotypically flamboyant and effeminate."

Roman's blue eyes didn't move away from his face. "But some are," he said. "And you seem to think there's something wrong with it. You're implying I'm homophobic. You're likely right. But I think you actually have more issues with your sexuality than I do. You say you're proud of being gay, but you're afraid to look gay."

"You don't know me," Luke managed through the lump in his throat, his breath coming in short gasps. His heart was pounding obnoxiously fast in his chest. Anxiety attack. He was having an anxiety attack. He had to calm down. It was easier said than done. God, he couldn't breathe. "You know nothing."

"Did I hit a nerve, kitten?" Roman said, stroking Luke's quivering bottom lip. He leaned to Luke's ear, his warm breath tickling him, and murmured, "You don't have to be manly with me, you know. You don't have to be anything. You can let go, sweetheart. Anything that happens here, stays here." He kissed the spot below Luke's ear, his rough beard scratching Luke's skin.

God.

Luke's eyes closed of their own volition. "Why are you doing this?" he whispered, trying to breathe, trying to pull himself together and failing. He was shaking, a wave of nausea overcoming him. He wanted to sag against Roman, let his forehead fall against his shoulder, and absorb his strength. "Why?" he said, trying to hold on to his sanity. "You want something."

"Of course I do," Roman said, running his fingers through Luke's hair. "But it doesn't mean I'm lying. I'm not going to judge you. I'm the last man who can judge anyone. You can let go, love. You can." He stroked Luke's cheek with his knuckles.

Luke all but mewled, leaning into Roman's touch, loving it and hating it. Why did this man affect him so easily? His proximity, his voice, his scent, his words.

Roman kissed behind his ear. Goosebumps broke out on Luke's skin. He whined, *needing*—needing this, needing to be touched, held and reassured.

"Shh. How about you get in my lap, love? You'll feel better."

Luke should have laughed in his face. Did Roman really think he didn't know how fake all these gentle touches and soft-spoken words were? Roman was just using his moment of weakness.

But he didn't laugh. He didn't resist when Roman pulled him on his lap. He buried his face against the top of Roman's chest, where his shirt was unbuttoned, the faintest tufts of chest hair tickling his nose, and breathed in and out, losing himself in the scent of a man, a healthy, fit man in his prime. A strong hand stroked his back, pulling him closer to the wide chest.

It felt so good, despite the warning bells ringing in the back of his mind.

Little by little, Luke's shaking subsided, his breathing evened out, clearing the fog surrounding his thoughts, and he started feeling self-conscious and embarrassed by his clingy mini-breakdown.

God, it had been years since he'd had an anxiety attack. He had thought he had outgrown them for good. Apparently not.

Luke pressed his cheek against Roman's chest. "Now what?" he said.

"Now you will tell me what kind of person Luke Whitford really is. Not the one you try to be. The real one."

His brows furrowing, Luke snorted. "So you can use it against me?"

"I have nothing against you, Curly," Roman said, tugging on a curl. "I have a problem with your father. He will pay for what he did. Not you."

"Then why am I here?" Luke said skeptically.

Roman took a moment to answer.

"Yes, I'm going to use you to achieve my goals," he said. "But I can give you my word that once this is over, you'll be back home, safe and unharmed."

A criminal's word should have meant very little. But Luke had a feeling Roman wasn't one to give his word lightly. It helped that Roman wasn't even bothering to deny that he was going to use him against his father.

"Why do you think I don't care about what happens to my father?"

"Do you?" Roman said.

Did he?

Luke thought about it—thought about the cold, distant man who had been mostly absent for most of his childhood.

"I don't hate him," Luke said. "I just don't know him. He's basically a stranger to me. So if you're hoping to get some dirt on him from me, don't waste your time." Luke laughed a little. "You probably know him better than I do." He smiled to himself, remembering all his failed attempts to get to know his father. "You asked who the real Luke Whitford is," he said quietly. "The thing is, I'm not sure. I'm a people-pleaser. I try to fit in every room I enter. In hindsight, maybe I did try to please my mother and be something she wanted, the same way I later tried to please my father and be the tough, manly heir he wanted—I don't know. I guess I've always just wanted to be enough." *But never was. I wish I could find someone who would love me the way I am and wouldn't want to change me.*

He didn't say it. Because the man he was talking to wasn't his friend, no matter how easy and good it felt to talk to him. The fact that he was sitting on Roman Demidov's lap, telling him his most intimate thoughts and letting the man *pet* his hair, was weird enough. He shouldn't—couldn't—trust this man. He shouldn't take comfort from Roman's hands or words, or the steady beat of his heart against Luke's ear.

"I don't know why I told you all of this," Luke said with a small laugh. "I don't know what I'm doing in your lap. Please do something evil soon. It's freaking me out how nice this feels."

Roman chuckled. "Maybe that's my evil plan," he said.

For all Luke knew, it could be.

It was a relief when Roman's phone went off. Reaching out, Roman pulled it out of his discarded jacket and answered, "Demidov." His voice was noticeably colder. Luke wasn't sure what to make of it.

"*Horosho. Ya budu tam skoro,*" Roman said and hung up.

He lifted Luke off his lap and put him back on the bed, as if he weighed nothing. "I have to go."

"Evil deeds to do, people to kidnap?" Luke said with a crooked smile.

"Something like that," Roman said, looking at his smile for a moment before leaning down and biting his cheek, teeth sinking into the flesh.

Luke flinched, more from surprise than any real pain.

"Um," he said, touching his cheek and trying to read Roman as the Russian stood up and slipped into his jacket.

One glance at Roman's crotch confirmed that Roman was half-hard. Luke looked up to find Roman watching him with an inscrutable expression.

Luke licked his lips, fisting the duvet in his fingers.

Roman chuckled. "Relax, *kotyonok*. I'm not going to touch you."

And then he was gone, leaving Luke with a strange feeling in his chest that felt too much like disappointment for his liking.

Roman didn't visit him again that day.

Later that night, Luke buried his head under his pillow, trying to ignore the high-pitched female moans coming from Roman's bedroom.

Chapter 10

Three days later, Luke stared moodily at the locked door of Roman's bedroom. He couldn't hear anything from the other side.

He lifted his hand and banged on the door, ignoring the voice in the back of his mind that told him he was crazy. He didn't care. He was exhausted and short-tempered from barely sleeping for the fourth night in a row.

It was all *his* fault.

The door opened and Luke found himself on the receiving end of a cold stare. Roman leaned a wide shoulder against the frame of the doorway, scrutinizing him from head to toe. He was wearing only a pair of black boxers, his dark hair tousled and a short, thick beard covering his square jaw.

Luke shifted from one foot to the other, looking anywhere but at Roman's bare chest and the tattoos on his muscular arms.

"Is there a reason you're banging on my door at six in the morning?" Roman said.

Luke crossed his arms over his chest. "I'm hungry."

"You're hungry," Roman repeated, somehow managing to convey how utterly unimportant the fact was to him without changing his expression.

"Yes," Luke said. "I haven't eaten anything since yesterday afternoon." He couldn't resist a glance over Roman's shoulder at the large bed dominating the room. It was empty, the sheets crumpled. "So your whore is gone," he said before he could stop himself.

He immediately regretted it as Roman's gaze sharpened, something like amusement appearing on his face. "Were you listening at the door, kitten?"

Luke glared at him. "I couldn't sleep all night because of her moans. For the fourth night in a row. And did you have to fuck her at three in the morning in our—in the bathroom we share?" Unable to look Roman in the eye any longer, he shifted his gaze to Roman's left ear. "I'm hungry, and I need something else to wear. The shirt you gave me feels gross already."

"It's endearing how you think you can disturb my sleep without a good enough reason," Roman said, a hint of steel appearing in his voice.

Luke froze, eyes flickering to Roman's. He swallowed.

Roman reached out, took the collar of Luke's shirt, and tugged him closer. Luke's heart thudded in his throat, his mouth dry.

"Or did you just want my attention, love?"

Flushing, Luke shook his head.

Of course he didn't want Roman's attention. He'd had plenty of it in the last three days. Every day, Roman would come to his room, talk to him about seemingly unrelated things, and just *watch* him.

It was kind of maddening, although Luke couldn't really complain that he was being mistreated. He had a soft bed, he was fed well enough, and the guards' beatings were a distant memory now. Roman didn't even touch him anymore. Frankly, Luke had little to complain about. As far as kidnappings went, this hadn't been that unpleasant of an experience—if only he hadn't been forced to listen to women orgasm every night.

Roman chuckled, his hand moving from Luke's shirt to his throat. His thumb pressed against Luke's madly beating pulse.

"Little liar," he said. "Did you come here because you were jealous of the nice woman who entertained me last night?"

Luke spluttered. "Jealous? I don't like you. You're a horrible, evil person."

"With cruel eyes," Roman added, amusement lacing his words. "Don't forget the cruel eyes."

"Don't make fun of me," Luke said, pouting.

It took him a moment to register that he was actually *pouting*. He blinked. What the hell. He'd always been very self-conscious about his facial expressions and rarely allowed himself to appear anything but masculine. When, exactly, had he let his guard down around Roman?

Feeling a little weirded out by his own behavior, Luke cleared his throat. "Fine, sorry for bothering you. Let go."

Roman's hand remained wrapped around his neck. He gave Luke a long, assessing look. Luke held his gaze, trying to ignore the proximity of his bare chest.

Looking him in the eye, Roman said quietly,

"Get on your knees."

Luke sucked in a sharp breath.

"No," he managed.

"Get on your knees," Roman repeated. "We both know this is what you came here for."

Wetting his lips, Luke glanced down at the bulge straining the fabric of Roman's black boxers. "No," he whispered, less sure than before.

"You should stop lying to yourself," Roman said. He buried his hand in Luke's hair and pushed him down, the pressure assertive and forceful, but not too forceful—just perfect—and a wave of arousal rolled through Luke.

Trembling, he waited on his knees, holding his breath. He could have moved away. He could move away.

He didn't.

He watched Roman pull himself out.

He didn't resist when Roman pried his mouth open with his fingers.

He didn't resist when Roman slowly fed him his fat cock.

Luke closed his eyes and moaned a little, relishing the way the hard, thick cock stretched his lips.

Roman wasn't slow or gentle. Immediately, his cock started pistoning in and out of Luke's mouth, bruising his throat and choking him, making Luke whimper around it. It went on, and on, Roman's low, guttural grunts the only sound in his ears.

There was a part of Luke that was ashamed by how much he got off on this: on being used like a hole for a cock, with no pretense of affection. For fuck's sake, he was sucking the cock of a man who saw nothing wrong with kidnapping people—who'd probably done things a lot worse than that. He was sick. Clearly he was sick to enjoy this, but he was *loving* this, loving this so much.

All too soon, Roman pulled on his hair roughly. Luke whined when the cock was pulled out of his mouth. No—

"Open your eyes."

He looked up and saw Roman already staring back at him. Roman tugged on his red, glistening cock, his eyes blazing with heat. "I'm going to come on your face. Open that pretty mouth for me, Curly."

Panting, Luke did as he was told, eyes fixed hungrily on the drops of pre-come at the tip of Roman's cock.

"*Blya*—" Roman grated out, stroking himself fast, and then he was coming all over Luke: his cheeks, his nose, his parted lips, down his neck and onto the shirt he was wearing.

"Fuck, look at you, angel," Roman said, running his hand through Luke's hair and pressing his face against Roman's thigh. "You may jerk off now."

Slipping his hand under his shirt, Luke grabbed his own dripping cock and groaned in relief. He was so hard it hurt. He wanked himself, panting against Roman's muscular thigh. He needed—

"Come on, love." Roman tugged on his hair, hard, and Luke was falling off the edge, teeth sinking into Roman's skin and his mind floating far, far away.

Leaning his forehead against Roman's thigh, he just breathed as those strong fingers continued stroking his curls, prolonging the pleasure coursing through his body. Luke was trying to make sense of what he was feeling, but all he could come up with was *warm* and *good*.

A distant part of him wondered what he was doing, what the fuck this was. This wasn't a normal behavior for him during sex. This giddy pliantness was anything but normal.

He would like to claim he was doing this to lull Roman into a false sense of security, but it would be kind of laughable. Now that he knew Roman a little better, Luke was sure a bit of cocksucking wouldn't make a difference. This man wasn't someone you could manipulate through sex. Roman fucked a different woman every night. If there was anyone being lulled into a false sense of security, it was Luke. He felt *safe* with Roman—at least safe enough to trust Roman with his body. How crazy was that?

"Stand up," Roman said.

Luke got to his feet unsteadily, his knees still weak, his body boneless.

Blue eyes studied him from his disheveled head to bare toes before Roman said, "Go take a shower. You're filthy."

Luke padded back to the bathroom. He really was filthy, his face covered in Roman's spunk. Besides, he didn't have any energy to argue. He didn't *want* to argue. Roman's authoritative tone didn't annoy him at all.

What's going on? he thought dazedly as he stood under the shower head, letting the water cascade down him.

By the time he turned the shower off, feeling clean and refreshed, his mind was clear of Roman-induced fog once again. Thank God. Lately his own mind freaked him out.

Shaking his head, Luke drew the shower screen aside and stopped.

Roman turned his head from the mirror. The hand that was trimming his beard went still as his eyes zeroed in on Luke's naked, wet body.

Luke took a few steps forward and stopped, reining in the insane urge to press his body against Roman's.

What the fuck, seriously.

A beat passed before Roman turned his gaze to the mirror again and returned to the task at hand. He was already partly dressed. It seemed he was leaving.

"You're dripping water on the floor," Roman said, wiping his face with a towel.

"I don't have anything to change into."

Roman went back into his bedroom.

"Come here," he called out when Luke didn't move.

Feeling a little self-conscious about his nudity, Luke did as he was told. Roman walked toward him, a pretty, patterned shirt in his hands.

Luke's eyebrows furrowed. The shirt was stylish and looked expensive, but he couldn't imagine it belonging to Roman. "It doesn't look at all like something you would wear."

"Because it isn't," Roman said. "It was a gift from—" He cut himself off and handed the shirt to Luke. "Put it on."

Luke did. When he was done buttoning it up, he turned to the mirror.

He stared.

He barely recognized the young man looking back at him. It'd been years since he let himself wear something so pretty and colorful. He looked...different, especially with his damp curls free from gel.

Stroking the soft, silky fabric, Luke found himself smiling a little at his reflection. His smile froze on his lips when he noticed that Roman was watching him.

Luke dropped his hand and coughed. "I look…
camp."

"Is that a bad thing?" Roman said.

Luke shrugged, unsure. Their conversation from the
other day was still fresh on his mind. He still didn't know
how he felt about it. Rationally, he knew Roman had been
right: there was nothing wrong with looking camp. It didn't
make him—or anyone else—a freak. But knowing
something rationally and believing it in your heart were
two different things.

Except that conversation *had* changed something.

*You don't have to be manly with me. You don't have to be
anything. You can let go. I'm the last man who can judge anyone.*

He wasn't sure he believed Roman, but…it didn't feel
wrong to wear something like this in Roman's presence. He
didn't feel self-conscious.

Luke couldn't stop glancing back at the mirror,
fascinated by how different he looked and felt. He didn't
look boring.

He looked…pretty. He felt pretty and interesting.

"You look nice."

Heat surging to his cheeks, Luke looked at Roman,
wide-eyed. There was no mocking edge to Roman's voice,
his tone matter-of-fact. He'd been complimented on his
looks plenty of times, but this felt different. Roman didn't
seem the type to give compliments freely.

"Thanks," Luke said awkwardly, feeling much too
flustered for his liking. He told himself not to be silly. It
was just a compliment, and not a fancy one.

But it wasn't *just* a compliment. He liked it because he
did feel lovely in this shirt, and he loved the feeling. Could
Roman see that? Was that why he'd said it?

Luke shot Roman a suspicious look, but the other man's face betrayed very little as he slipped into a gray shirt and started buttoning it up.

Luke looked at the packed suitcase by the bed and chewed his lip. *Are you leaving?*

He didn't ask.

"Are you going to give me some trousers anytime soon?" he asked instead.

"No," Roman said, glancing at his legs. "You're tiny. You'd trip over your feet if I gave you mine."

Luke frowned. He wasn't tiny. Though, to Roman, who was built like a tank, he probably did look tiny. "You could give me someone else's."

"No."

"What about some underwear?

"No."

Luke let out a long-suffering sigh. "Are you going to tell me when I'm going home?"

"No."

Pursing his lips, Luke plopped down on Roman's bed and looked at the suitcase again.

Roman glanced at him and snorted. "Stop making that face and go back to your room."

"I'm beginning to feel like your pet." Luke was really starting to wonder what he was to Roman. Why was Roman doing this? Despite his generally stern attitude, he seemed noticeably softer around Luke lately, and, as a result, Luke found himself dropping his guard. A week ago, he wouldn't have dared speak to Roman in such a sullen tone. A week ago, he had been scared shitless of the guy. Now he was getting too comfortable with him and, the strangest thing was, Roman was *letting* him.

Roman had been almost nice to him. Why? Why, why, why?

God, he'd never been so confused in his life. This man was a walking contradiction. Roman seemed vaguely homophobic, but at the same time he was very open-minded and understanding when it came to sex. He was domineering as hell, but, unlike most overbearing men, he was a good listener and easy to talk to. Roman wasn't gay but was attracted to him. Luke had no idea what to make of it all. It didn't seem like Roman was pretending—some things were impossible to fake—but he was sure Roman was playing some game. He must be.

Roman grabbed his suitcase. "Whatever gave you that idea? A pet wouldn't ask so many questions and pout when I don't answer them."

"I never pout," Luke said, pouting exaggeratedly, though he was unsure why. "It's my lips. I'm going to get plastic surgery to fix them."

Roman's dark brows drew together. He eyed Luke's lips.

Luke moistened them with the tip of his tongue.

"There's nothing to fix," Roman said shortly and started turning away.

"Are you leaving?" Luke blurted out.

Roman paused and gave him a long, probing look.

"Yes," he said after a moment. "Work. There's only so much I can do from Russia. I won't be back until next Thursday."

"You'll be gone for a week?" Luke frowned. "But—but who will feed me?" He didn't know why, but Roman didn't allow any of his men to enter Luke's room while Roman wasn't there.

"Vlad will," Roman said, something cold flashing in his eyes. "He will behave." He gave Luke a considering look. Then, he walked over and, sinking his fingers into Luke's hair, held his gaze with an odd sort of intensity. "He will only bring you food. He's not allowed to stay in the room longer than necessary. Understood?"

Confused, Luke nodded nevertheless. "Why are you telling *me* that? It's not like I can kick him out."

"I've had a talk with him," Roman said, something faintly displeased about his expression. "But you can always remind him of my orders if he forgets about them."

His eyes dropped to Luke's mouth again. The grip on his curls tightened.

Luke's heart started pounding. His face tilted up, his lips parting. Fuck, he wanted to be kissed so, so badly. He wanted to feel that beard against his chin. He wanted Roman's tongue in his mouth.

Roman let go and stepped away.

Deflating, Luke watched numbly as Roman strode out of the room.

The door locked after him with an audible click.

Luke plopped back on Roman's bed and groaned in frustration, touching his tingling lips.

"You're such an idiot, Luke," he said aloud before laughing.

It was either that or crying.

Chapter 11

"I told you to stay out of this room," Vlad said when he brought him food.

Luke took the tray and ignored his words.

In the past six days since Roman had left, he had perfected the art of ignoring Roman's head of security. It wasn't difficult. He didn't know what Roman had told Vlad, but these days the beefy blond barely dared look at him when he brought him food.

It was kind of funny how carefully Vlad avoided any eye contact. It was a stark contrast to the way the guy had behaved before: the look in Vlad's eyes had used to make Luke uncomfortable whenever Vlad had visited him. Now the guy barely glanced his way, even when he scowled and berated Luke for something.

"He'll be angry if he comes back and finds you here," Vlad persisted.

Luke shrugged. "He should have locked the room from my side, then," he said, turning on the TV and making himself comfortable against the pillows. The TV was the main reason he had been hanging out here more often than in his own room, choosing to ignore Vlad's disapproval when he caught him in Roman's room for the first time several days ago.

Although most channels were Russian, it was such a relief to have something to take his mind off the situation he was in — and the boredom gnawing at his senses.

Luke was a social person. He'd never been all that good at entertaining himself, and *nothing* had been happening.

Sometimes he would see the guards laughing, drinking, and exchanging dirty jokes in the backyard. Sometimes he would hear distant sounds of drunken songs and laughter through the door. It seemed that with the boss gone, Roman's men became far too relaxed and undisciplined. They never behaved that way when Roman was in the house. Luke was positive that if he hadn't been locked up, he could have slipped away unnoticed. He could have escaped.

"You aren't supposed to be here," Vlad said.

Luke poured himself some coffee and sipped it, studying Vlad over the rim of his mug. He knew Vlad wanted him; he had noticed it from the first day. He was pretty sure Vlad was latent homosexual. He did consider using Vlad to escape, but the idea of seducing him turned his stomach. He couldn't do it. Not only was he not attracted to the guy in the least, but he also felt anything but safe with him. Unlike Roman, Vlad could be violent without any reason. Luke remembered the sadistic gleam in his eyes when Vlad had watched the guards rough him up.

He had to be careful.

"I'm pretty sure it's you who isn't supposed to be here," Luke said calmly. "You're supposed to bring me food and then go. Your boss wouldn't be pleased to find out you're disobeying his orders."

Luke couldn't deny it felt good to know that Roman's orders were protecting him. Obviously Roman had some ulterior motives for giving such orders, but the fact remained that Vlad could do nothing to him. And they both knew it.

Vlad scowled and stormed out, muttering in Russian that Luke was going to regret it once Roman returned.

Luke frowned. Truth be told, he wasn't all that sure Vlad was wrong. Strictly speaking, Roman hadn't explicitly allowed him to hang out in his bedroom. Roman had simply left him in this room after…

Sighing, Luke set his mug down and started channel-surfing, trying to ignore the restless feeling under his skin. The time was dragging so slowly. It was Wednesday; Roman wasn't supposed to be back until tomorrow, and Luke felt itchy with impatience. It was just…He felt like he was stuck in limbo, waiting for any news from the outside world. It had been almost three weeks since his kidnapping, and he had so many questions and no answers.

He kept wondering what was happening to his family and friends. He was worried about James: his friend had been far too depressed to be left alone for such a long time. Was James even eating? And surely Luke's father must know by now that he had been kidnapped. Had he been contacted already? His mother? Was there any ransom demand?

It wouldn't make any sense, though. Roman didn't exactly need money. He was filthy rich, his official net worth making him one of the wealthiest men in Eastern Europe (and Luke had little doubt his official net worth wasn't anywhere close to his actual net worth).

But if it wasn't money Roman was after, why was Luke even here? Sure, the whole kidnapping thing could be a simple act of revenge against his father, but Luke hadn't been harmed, so what was the point? Yes, prior to Roman's arrival, his men roughed him up a bit, but Luke didn't think it was on Roman's orders. Or was it? Was Roman just playing some elaborate mind-game?

Fuck, it was all so bewildering and frustrating—even without taking into account the…the thing between him and Roman that was becoming hard to ignore.

Twice. It had happened twice already.

It wasn't even the blowjobs that bothered Luke. It was the attraction, the sheer strength of it, the almost slavish intensity of that pull. What should one call attraction to a cold, manipulative man one didn't even like? A case of stupid.

Luke laughed out loud. Yeah, definitely. It was so stupid. He had *promised* himself he was done getting involved with assholes. He had promised. He wanted to meet a nice guy, fall in love, and start a family with him. A real family. A husband. Lots of kids. A nice, cozy house filled with laughter, joy, and love. James called him a hopeless sap, but Luke wasn't ashamed of his dreams. Having grown up with a distant father and a mother who had lived separately for most of his life, Luke had always yearned for a home and family.

Being gay complicated everything a little—or a lot, considering what a homophobe his father was—but Luke refused to give up on his dream. It was the twenty-first century. Gay people could get married in some countries. There were ways to have children, too: adoption, surrogacy. His dreams were achievable.

He just had to find a nice man to build a life with—and stop getting hung up on assholes.

Luke smiled crookedly. So far he was doing a fantastic job. Roman made all his ex-boyfriends seem like saints in comparison. His exes were just assholes; they weren't even in the same league as Roman, who actually did things like kidnap people—and probably things far worse than that. And yet he let the guy touch him and shove his dick down his throat whenever Roman wanted. Hell, he had been eager for that. It was so embarrassing, even by his pitiful standards. James would call him an idiot and be absolutely right.

Sighing, Luke focused his attention on the TV screen. It was showing an episode of Masha and The Bear. He had seen it before with his goddaughter, Camila, but for some reason, the cartoon was a lot funnier in Russian, and Luke found himself giggling at Masha's silly antics.

"What are you doing here?"

Luke's grin slipped from his face.

* * *

Roman barely paid attention to Vlad's report as he strode toward his room. He was exhausted after the flight and all he wanted was his bed.

"Later, Vlad," he said, punching the code in on the keypad and pushing the door open.

He went still at the sight that greeted him.

Luke was sprawled on his bed, giggling at something on the TV, his curls in disarray, dimples framing his mouth. He was wearing a violet t-shirt—Roman hadn't even known he owned something that color—that had ridden up to his thighs.

"What are you doing here?" Roman heard himself say.

Luke turned his head and stared at him, his grin fading.

Before the boy could respond, Vlad, who still stood behind Roman, cut in hurriedly in Russian, "Look, I told the brat to leave, but he didn't obey. He—"

"Get out," Roman said, his eyes trained on Luke.

Pursing his lips, the boy sat up, but Roman bit off, "I'm talking to you, Vlad. You're dismissed."

A beat passed before Vlad nodded and left. Roman stepped inside, letting the door close, the lock engaging.

They were alone now.

After a moment, Luke shifted his gaze back to the TV, staring at it with a great deal of interest—perhaps with too much interest for that to be genuine. Roman followed his gaze and only then realized what Luke was watching.

"You're watching cartoons," Roman said flatly.

He dropped his suitcase on the chair and started unbuttoning his jacket, but his gaze kept returning to the boy still lounging in his bed. His t-shirt was too big on Luke, leaving his creamy neck and collarbone exposed. Despite Roman's exhaustion, his cock twitched and started thickening.

Roman gritted his teeth, irritated by his body's reaction to this boy once again.

"I love cartoons," Luke said lightly. His hand, Roman noticed, was gripping the duvet.

"You love cartoons," Roman said. "Are you an actual child?"

"Don't be so narrow-minded," Luke said, keeping his eyes on the screen. "We all have a little bit of kid inside of us. I love kids, and I love cartoons. They can teach us valuable lessons." He smiled a little.

He was fucking ridiculous. Whitford couldn't have possibly produced this strange boy.

"I have a goddaughter," Luke volunteered, breaking the silence. "I'd love to have my own kids someday."

"You?" Roman didn't bother to hide his amusement.

Luke finally dragged his eyes from the screen to glare at him. A disgruntled kitten, indeed. "Yes, me. What's so funny?"

"You're a baby yourself," Roman said, taking him in from head to bare toes.

"Appearances can be misleading," Luke said, flushing. "I'll have you know I'm great with babies. It's always been my dream to have a big family, have lots of kids." He hesitated before adding, "And a loving husband."

Roman felt his lips curl in distaste.

"What?" Luke said, his chin lifting. He turned the TV off. "You think there's something wrong with it? With being gay?"

"With being gay? Personally, I never got the appeal, but I don't care what people get off to. Different strokes." Roman loosened his tie. "But don't you think it's unnatural to want a family with a man?"

There was something objectionable about the idea of

Luke having a "loving husband."

He didn't like it.

Luke cocked his head to the side, his fringe falling into his brown eyes. "I understand why you might feel that way," he said, his voice soft. "I know homophobia is more prominent in Russian society than in England. But you're wrong. There's documented evidence of homosexual behavior in animals, too. So it's not unnatural. Just different from the norm."

The boy's fingers were still clenched.

"You aren't as blasé about it as you pretend," Roman said, unbuttoning his shirt.

"I'm not," Luke admitted with a crooked smile. "I already told you about my dad's views. I tried hard to be 'normal' to make him happy. I changed the way I dressed and the way I acted, but I couldn't change what I wanted, no matter how hard I tried to like girls. And I tried. But eventually, I gave up. I like men. I've made peace with it. If I was born that way, it can't be wrong or unnatural."

"Why don't you tell that to your father, then?"

Luke dropped his gaze and shrugged, his t-shirt slipping off his shoulder. "I'm…Okay, yeah, I'm scared of his reaction." He bit the inside of his cheek. "I'm not ready to come out to him. I guess he will find out when I meet the man of my dreams and decide to settle down."

Roman shrugged his shirt off. "The man of your dreams," he said, not bothering to hide the mockery in his voice. "And who is that?"

Luke's fingers stroked his bare thigh, more of a nervous gesture than anything else, his long eyelashes almost touching his creamy skin.

"I don't know," he said slowly.

"I guess I'll recognize him when I see him. Obviously he must be attractive, and he must have the balls to stand up to my father. But first and foremost, he must be good-natured and nice. He must love kids and want the same things as me." A faint blush tinted his cheeks. "And he must adore me, of course."

Of course.

Roman threw his shirt in the laundry basket.

Flinching, Luke looked up. His gaze swept over Roman's bare chest before meeting his eyes. The silence stretched, taut and tangible.

"You look…angry," Luke murmured.

"I'm never angry," Roman said.

That was true, to an extent. He couldn't remember the last time he showed his anger outwardly. Any strong emotion was a potential weakness he couldn't afford to display. He had distanced himself from the majority of his family for a reason. They were safer that way. It was easier that way for him, too.

"You returned early," Luke said. "Did something happen? Is there any news?"

His dark eyes were wide and beautiful, and his lips looked soft and very pink. It was irritating. Everything about the boy irritated him: the way he looked, the way he talked, the way he fucking breathed.

Roman felt his jaw clench.

In a few long strides, he crossed the distance between them and yanked the boy up by the collar of his shirt. "Do you think you're a guest here?"

Luke blinked slowly.

"No?" he said, his voice still irritatingly soft and musical, even as his breathing became unsteady.

"You seem to think you're entitled to answers," Roman said, only a few inches separating them. "That I owe you any explanation."

"I…" Luke said, looking a little flustered. He stared at Roman, the expression on his face earnest and open. "I just want to know why I'm here—what you want with me. I think that's fair, don't you think?"

Fair?

"I think," Roman said, letting his voice acquire an edge he reserved for dealing with enemies he had every intention of crushing. "I think I've been too soft with you."

Luke's Adam's apple moved. Biting his lip, he shook his head.

"No?" Roman said, amused despite himself.

A dimple appearing in his cheek, the boy shook his head again, his curls framing his heart-shaped face like a halo. It wasn't endearing. At all.

More than a little annoyed, Roman dug the fingers of his free hand into Luke's hip. Luke inhaled shakily, his pupils blowing wide.

"For a fairy boy who dreams of nice men and sappy romance, you sure like it rough," Roman said.

Luke flushed. "For a homophobic man, you sure like groping me. Are you sure you aren't a 'fairy' too?"

When he was touching this boy, he wasn't sure of a damn thing.

Roman said mildly, "Is that supposed to offend me? Besides, if I let you suck my dick a few times, it doesn't mean I'm into men. You have blowjob lips. That's all."

Something shattered in Luke's expression, the look in his eyes becoming fragile and hurt. Unease curled low in Roman's stomach. It only made him angrier.

For fuck's sake.

He never cared about hurting people, much less about hurting people's feelings.

"Okay," Luke said, averting his gaze. "Fair enough. I've been told that before."

Roman's lips thinned.

"Let go, please," Luke said softly, still not looking at him. "I get it: I'm nothing but a pawn for you, and I shouldn't expect to be treated like a person. I got it. I get it—"

Roman grabbed his head and kissed him, pouring his anger into the greedy kiss.

Damn you. This wasn't how it was supposed to go. Yes, he had fully intended to fuck with Luke's mind, make him dependent on him and need him. He'd already half-conditioned the boy to want Roman's attention, his kisses and his cock. He had fully intended to kiss the boy at some point after his return—*days* later—after making Luke wonder and second-guess himself.

He wasn't supposed to be licking the boy's mouth with his tongue as soon as he returned. He wasn't supposed to think of Luke's mouth and skin during business meetings. And he sure as hell wasn't supposed to rush back from the airport like a hormonal teenager, impatient to get his hands on the boy.

Luke was rigid for exactly four seconds before going deliciously pliant against his chest and starting to suck on Roman's tongue with muffled moans that went straight to Roman's cock. Luke's responsiveness was beyond arousing, washing all his reservations away and making him greedy and hungry.

He wanted to fucking destroy this ridiculous boy,

with his irritating dimples and ridiculous lips, with his soft smiles and soft voice, with his silly, sappy dreams. He wanted to wreck him, take him apart, and put a collar on him with Roman's—

Breathing hard, Roman wrenched his mouth away, dropping Luke back on the bed.

What the fuck.

He took a few deep breaths before finally looking at Luke. He lay, panting, on Roman's bed, his lips wet and swollen, his eyes glossy with desire, his cock tenting the fabric of his shirt. The latter should have been a turn-off, but it had the opposite effect.

I want to fuck him.

The strength of that desire was startling.

He'd told Luke the truth: although he didn't consider himself a raging homophobe, Roman could never before understand the appeal of fucking men. Hairy, flat chests simply held no appeal to him. Even fucking a man's mouth was one thing—a wet mouth really was just a wet mouth— but engaging in anal sex with a man was a different matter entirely. He'd never thought he would want it.

And yet, as he looked down at the young man sprawled out in his bed, flushed, beautiful and aroused, all Roman wanted was to climb on top of him, push his legs apart, shove his cock inside him, and fuck him for hours. For days.

He didn't know what was written on his face, but Luke let out a laugh that sounded more like a groan. "No way. Forget about it," he said hoarsely, his eyes dark and bottomless. "I'm done letting straight assholes fuck me over."

Roman retrieved a bottle of lube and condoms from

the bedside drawer. He tossed the bottle to Luke. "You know what to do."

The boy opened and closed his mouth before glaring at him. His glares were about as effective as a kitten's. He was *lovely*. Roman wanted to stick his cock in his every hole.

"I don't want this," Luke whispered. "If you want it, you'll have to force me."

Roman thumbed open the button of his fly. "I'm not in the mood to play that game tonight." His gaze roamed over Luke's smooth legs, his cock aching as he imagined them wrapped around his waist. "Let's drop the bullshit, shall we? I want to fuck you. You want me to fuck you, even though I'm not the nice man you want to have babies with."

He sneered at that, his irritation spiking. "Prep yourself," he said. He could do it himself, but the less he touched the boy, the better. Touching him was fucking addictive, and nicotine was the only addiction he allowed himself.

Luke licked his lips. "And what if I don't?"

"You'll go to your room, and I'll find a nice, willing woman to take your place," Roman said, shrugging and pulling his zipper down. "No difference for me." It was a lie. He didn't want a hole to fuck. He wanted to fuck *this* boy, feel him come apart under him, on his cock.

A beat passed, then another.

When Luke reached for the lube, Roman's body tensed, blood rushing to his cock.

He tore his eyes away and resumed undressing, keeping his movements unhurried. It wouldn't do to show impatience.

He'd made enough mistakes already. Fucking Whitford's son this evening hadn't been in his plans. Fucking him hadn't been in his plans, full stop.

Only once he was completely naked, he put on a condom and allowed himself to look back at Luke.

Shit.

Luke's shirt had ridden up to his chest, revealing the creamy skin of his stomach, his hard cock, his shapely, strong thighs, and slim, toned legs that were surprisingly long despite his average height. His pink hole was glistening with lube, taking three fingers easily. He was a sight to behold: all flushed and pretty, an innocent angel and a whore.

Dark, glazed eyes met his. Luke bit his bottom lip and started moving his fingers harder and deeper, looking at Roman from under his eyelashes and panting.

"Stop," Roman said, lubing himself up. His balls were aching already, sweat beading on his brow. "Fingers out."

Luke pulled out his fingers and sighed, squirming, his hole pulsing around nothing. He stared at Roman's thick erection with what could only be described as hunger, his pupils blown.

"Shirt off. On your hands and knees," Roman said, squeezing the base of his cock. It wasn't really what he wanted. He wanted to fuck the boy on his back, holding his wrists down and kissing his pretty mouth. He wanted to watch his every reaction and see his face when he came. That was why he wouldn't do it. The less personal it was, the better.

Luke got on all fours and arched his bare back, his perky ass up in the air.

Fucking hell.

Roman knelt behind him and gripped his hips, watching the milky skin redden under his fingers.

He could still stop.

He was about to fuck a man. He was about to stick his cock in another man's asshole.

He didn't want to stop.

"This is a terrible idea," Luke whispered, his voice catching.

"It is," Roman agreed before slowly pushing his cock in.

They both grunted, Roman gritting his teeth as incredible tightness enveloped his cock. The urge to move, the urge to *take* was irresistible.

He didn't move.

He stayed still, sweat dripping down his forehead.

Luke whined, sounding dazed already.

"Move," he whispered, squirming. "Please."

"No," Roman said. "If you want to be fucked, you'll have to work for it."

"I don't understand," Luke said, sounding frustrated as he shifted his hips impatiently.

Roman chuckled hoarsely and pulled out until only the tip remained inside, his eyes locked on where their bodies were connected. His cock looked obscenely huge and red between the boy's pale cheeks. "Fuck yourself on my cock, *kotyonok*. Take what you need."

Luke made a small sound. He braced himself on the pillow, sucking in breaths, and then slammed his hips back.

Roman hissed but remained still, watching Luke fuck himself the way he liked it. He didn't angle his hips at all, leaving it up to Luke to twist and squirm in order to hit his sweet spot.

Soon, Luke was impaling himself on his cock with feverish intensity, setting a brutal rhythm for them that sent the headboard knocking against the wall as he rocked back onto Roman's cock over and over, panting and whimpering a little.

Roman gritted his teeth. He could see that the boy was getting tired, his breathing becoming harsher, his arms and thighs shaking with exertion. It took all his self-control not to thrust his hips, deeper into the tight heat.

"Please," Luke said, nearly sobbing as his arms gave out. "Please."

Roman leaned down, so that his chest was pressing against Luke's back, so that he was completely covering him, and then he snapped his hips forward. Luke let out a happy sound and relaxed as Roman took charge, pounding into him and grinding him into the mattress with every thrust.

"Oh God." Luke wasn't very loud, but he let out a nearly constant string of moans as Roman rocked his hips into him mercilessly, loving the view of his cock disappearing into Luke's stretched hole.

"Enjoying yourself?" Roman grunted, mouthing the back of the boy's neck. He liked how small Luke was, his body easily accessible everywhere. "Look at you, getting fucked by a man who kidnapped you, and enjoying it." He bit the boy's earlobe. "Such a slutty little thing. Isn't that right, *suchka*?" He dragged his cock out and slammed back in.

Luke whimpered, burying his face in the pillow and lifting his ass higher.

"Yeah," he mumbled. "Don't stop."

Roman didn't stop. He wasn't sure he even could, all his senses narrowing to the boy's tight hole around his throbbing cock, and Luke's wantons moans and groans. The boy *was* a whore for cock; he was truly getting off on being fucked roughly, his moans increasing in volume with each thrust, each time Roman called him something derogatory. Such a kinky little thing.

Dazedly, Roman wondered if his people could hear Luke's moans, if they could guess that their boss was fucking the male captive.

Let them hear. He wanted them to hear. He wanted everyone to know how much the boy was enjoying being nailed on his cock.

"Please—please," Luke croaked between his moans as Roman kept his relentless pace. "Touch me. Need it."

Sliding his hand under Luke, Roman wrapped it around his cock and gave a few tugs, thrusting hard inside him. Luke cried out and came, his hole clenching around Roman's cock.

He shook for a long while, stunned and fucked-out, and Roman fucked him through his orgasm, chasing his own, low grunts escaping his throat. Luke was boneless under him, panting as Roman's cock pistoned in and out of him. Almost there—

Burying his face in Luke's damp curls, Roman bit at his nape and thrust a few more times, groaning as he spilled inside the condom.

He remained still on top of the slim body for a long while, steading his ragged breathing.

At last, he pulled out, rolled off and flopped onto his back, his chest heaving. He tied the condom and threw it in the direction of the trash can.

Luke shifted beside him and burrowed into Roman's side, pressing his cheek against Roman's biceps.

Roman stiffened.

He turned his head. Luke had his eyes half-closed, his face still flushed, his golden curls darker with sweat, a hint of a smile on his plump lips. Roman could barely believe this was the same boy who got off on being slut-shamed and called homophobic names. He looked like a sleepy, satisfied kitten. He looked sated and happy.

Roman wanted to push him away.

He didn't, of course.

This was good. This was excellent, actually. This meant he hadn't completely messed up his plans. Roman could put up with some post-coital snuggling if that was what the boy needed.

"You're a good lay," Luke said sleepily, fingers playing with the sparse dark hair on Roman's chest. "For a straight, homophobic prick."

Roman buried his hand in Luke's hair. "And how many straight, homophobic pricks have you fucked?"

"You're not the first," Luke mumbled, leaning into his touch.

Roman tugged on a curl.

"What?" Luke murmured, looking at him. His eyes were still glazed and soft. "You think you're the first straight guy led astray by my 'blowjob lips'?" Luke smiled, but there was an edge to it.

Someone had hurt him in the past.

"Led astray?" Roman said. "I'm a grown man, sweetheart. I'm fully responsible for my actions. A pretty mouth isn't enough to sway me if I don't let it."

Luke looked at him a little uncertainly.

"I fucked you because I wanted it," Roman clarified, looking him in the eye. "Simple as that. Anyone who claims otherwise is a spineless coward."

Luke chuckled. "Please, stop making sense. You're the villain. Don't deviate from the script."

"Even villains are allowed to have a few semi-redeeming moments."

"Not you," Luke said, smiling sleepily. "You're supposed to be a royal dickhead all the time."

"Yeah?" Roman said, eyeing the deep dimple in the boy's cheek.

"Yep," Luke said solemnly before yawning. "Think I'm gonna sleep here," he muttered, closing his eyes.

"Really," Roman said, looking at him in disbelief. No one simply invited themselves into his bed. People knew better.

"If you want me to leave, you'll have to carry me to my room," Luke mumbled. "My legs always feel like jelly after a good shag. So it's your fault."

"Aren't you scared of me anymore?" Roman said, feeling more amused than annoyed, to his own surprise.

Luke opened his eyes and looked at him seriously.

"You do scare me sometimes," he said, his voice quiet. "I know you're not a good person. I know you're capable of horrible things. But physically, I feel safe with you—right now. It might change, though." He smiled a little. "I'm not naive enough to think you won't hurt me if you decide it will benefit you."

Roman stared at him. The boy kept surprising him. He wasn't wrong: Roman had no interest in hurting him. Not at the moment.

"You may stay," he said finally.

Nodding, Luke slung an arm over Roman's chest and snuggled in closer. "I love cuddles," he said, yawning. "Don't take it personally. All people I fuck know it's something they'll have to put up with afterward. I'm the biggest cuddle monster you'll ever meet." He closed his eyes. "Good night."

"Good night, cuddle monster," Roman said wryly and reached out to turn the light off, leaving on only the dim bedside lamp.

He breathed evenly for a while, trying to distance himself from the warm male body pressed to his side, from the soft curls his fingers were still tangled in.

He'd just had sex with a man.

Roman waited, but the feeling of wrongness he half-expected to feel never came. The sex had been good. More than good.

Shaking the thought off, he focused on his plans.

The boy was almost his.

Almost.

Turning his head, Roman looked at Luke. He was sleeping like a baby, foolishly oblivious to what a monster he was snuggled up to.

Chapter 12

Luke couldn't breathe.

Or rather, he could, but every breath took a great deal of effort, because his face was buried in the pillow and he was crushed under something big and heavy.

Before panic could settle in his sleepy mind, a familiar scent hit his nostrils. Roman. Of course it was him.

Luke breathed out and then almost laughed. The whole thing was bizarre. Relief was the last thing he should have been feeling in this situation. He couldn't be that stupid to think he was safe with this man, regardless of the fantastic dicking he'd gotten last night.

Thinking of last night certainly didn't help his morning wood. It also didn't help that Roman's beard scratched the sensitive skin of his cheek every time he breathed. And was that…? Yep, the hard length pressed against his ass was unmistakable.

Biting his lip, Luke listened. Roman was still asleep, his breathing steady and slow. He was sprawled mostly on top of Luke, heavy and firm in all the right places. His body was all muscle, a body of a *man* in his prime, not at all like the bodies of guys his own age Luke usually slept with.

God, it was all so very unfair. Luke had always had a bit of a thing for fit older men, assholes, authority figures, men who looked like they could crush you and not break into a sweat—and Roman was all of those things. It was as though Roman was a perfect blend of all the wrong traits Luke shouldn't be drawn to but was.

He shouldn't have let Roman fuck him. He should have left when Roman had given him the choice; Luke knew that. Except he hadn't wanted to spend another night listening to some woman's moans. *He* was the one who had given Roman that erection. It was his.

Great. Apparently now he was getting possessive over the guy's erection. It wasn't weird at all.

Luke squirmed a little, trying to dislodge Roman and get out of bed, but it was an exercise in futility. Not only hadn't he managed that, but all the squirming only turned him on and Luke found himself flushed and panting raggedly under Roman's body, unsure whether he wanted to get up after all or not. Scratch that, of course he wanted to—he could barely breathe, and he was sticky inside and out—but his traitorous, silly body was perfectly content to remain where it was, underneath the man who had him kidnapped for god-knows-what reasons.

He squirmed again half-heartedly and his breath caught in his throat when Roman's erection poked between his cheeks, catching on the rim of his hole.

Roman grunted and tensed up against him, his breathing no longer steady.

Teeth scraped Luke's neck.

"*Hochu yobnut tebya, kudryashka*," Roman said in Russian, his voice still hoarse from sleep. "*Hochu trahnut tebya bez rezinki.*"

Luke shuddered. He hadn't understood everything Roman had said, but the general gist was pretty clear: Roman wanted to fuck him without a condom, and he had used some of the filthiest Russian words for "fuck." It wasn't the words that shocked him; it was the fact that Luke wanted it, too, and *that* shook him to his core. Sex without a condom was the deepest form of intimacy, something that required complete trust in your partner. Luke never let anyone fuck him without one. Wanting it with this man was pure madness. Was he crazy?

Deeply uncomfortable, Luke muttered, "You're crushing me."

After a moment, Roman rolled off him and lay on his side, propping himself up on an elbow.

Breathing out, Luke turned his head to him. Roman was regarding him intently, his blue eyes still a little hazy from sleep, dark beard framing his square jaw. Luke wondered how that beard would feel against his thighs.

"Don't even think about it," he said, trying not to ogle Roman's wide shoulders and muscular chest too blatantly. "I'm not letting you fuck me without a condom. I never let anyone do that."

A corner of Roman's mouth twitched. "Is that honor reserved for your nice man?"

There definitely was a mocking edge to his voice when he had said the word "nice."

Luke scowled. "Maybe, maybe not. But a man who has a new woman every night definitely doesn't get to do it."

The bastard actually grinned. "You're cute when you get jealous." Before Luke could tell him how ridiculous it was, Roman leaned in and licked the corner of Luke's lips.

"Go brush your teeth. I want to kiss your pretty mouth."

"Your morning breath doesn't exactly smell like roses, either," Luke grumbled, though Roman's morning breath was fine.

"Evil men get leeway," Roman said, his face dead serious. "It's in the 'How to Be Evil For Dummies.' Latest edition."

Luke couldn't stop a giggle.

Roman stared at him with a strange expression. "You have thirty seconds to brush your teeth, Curly. Then you're going to return here, suck on my tongue, and sit on my cock."

It was rather embarrassing how fast Luke rolled out of the bed and made a beeline for the bathroom.

At least, Luke consoled himself later, he had enough willpower to insist on a condom.

It was a small comfort.

Chapter 13

"Remind Sergei to seal the deal with Gazprom as soon as possible," Roman said, without looking up from his computer. "I expect a detailed report by the end of the month. Any news from Anna?"

Vlad hesitated, wondering if he should tell Roman how surprised Anna was by his absence from the negotiations. Normally, Roman was something of a control freak.

But then again, nothing was fucking normal around here these days.

"She's doing everything she can," Vlad replied, deciding against it. Roman's moods could be unpredictable. "She says the negotiations are going reasonably well."

Roman hummed. "Anything else?"

"We've had a few inquiries from the British Secret Intelligence Service."

Roman lifted his gaze. "Again?"

Vlad nodded, frowning. "They don't seem suspicious—they have nothing on us—but they're requesting a meeting with you. By all accounts, you were the last person Luke Whitford met before his disappearance a month ago."

"I have already told everything I know to the Russian police," Roman said, leveling him with a flat look. "The SIS can ask them. Why are you bothering me with this?"

Vlad pursed his lips. "Don't you think you should agree to meet them? To dispel any suspicion?"

"I'm the CEO of multiple corporations all over the world," Roman said slowly, as if speaking to a small child. "My schedule is booked months in advance. It would be far too suspicious if I agreed to an unofficial request, considering that I supposedly barely know the missing person and spent a total of five minutes in his company. I have a bullet-proof alibi."

"Yes, but…Maybe Whitford has told them about the bad blood between you two," Vlad said. "If he has, they'll know you have a motive."

"Richard Whitford will lose far more than me if he talks," Roman said before returning his gaze to the computer. "You may go."

When Vlad didn't move, Roman looked up again. "Anything else?"

Vlad bit the inside of his cheek.

"I don't have all day, Vlad," Roman said.

"It's been over a month since we got the boy," Vlad said, haltingly. "And you haven't used him yet."

Roman bored his pale eyes into him.

Vlad swallowed, reminding himself that he was the closest thing Roman had to a friend after Misha's death.

"Are you asking me to explain myself to you?" Roman said at last, his voice low and seemingly casual.

Vlad knew better.

"Not at all," he said quickly. "It's just…I'm worried. The longer we keep him here, the bigger the security risk.

At least let me ship him off to a more distant, secure location—maybe the safe house near Omsk or—"

"No."

Vlad waited, but when no further explanation was provided, he gritted his teeth. It wasn't as though he thought he was entitled to know all of Roman's plans, but this issue was actually his job. He was supposed to be informed of any potential security risks, and the boy currently locked up in Roman's rooms was going to become a bigger security risk the longer he stayed in the house just outside Saint Petersburg.

While Vlad was confident in his men's loyalty, he didn't delude himself into thinking that leaks were impossible.

"But," he tried again. "The boy—"

Roman stared him down. "The boy is none of your concern. Dismissed."

Nodding tightly, Vlad left the room.

Once he was back in the control center, he sat in his chair and looked blankly at the security feeds.

After a moment, he keyed a passcode into the datapad and brought up the security feed for Whitford boy's room.

The kid was sprawled on the bed, reading a book. Vlad frowned; he didn't think there had been books in that room.

He stared at the screen some more, disconcerted by how comfortable the boy looked for someone who was a captive. Vlad was about to close the security feed when the boy suddenly looked up from his book, toward the door.

Roman entered the room and said something.

There was no audio, so Vlad could only guess what was being said.

Luke responded and, pursing his lips, returned his eyes to the book. Discarding his jacket, Roman walked to the bed and tipped the boy's head up. Whitford's brat glared at him, lips folding into a pout.

Vlad's jaw dropped when the boy practically jumped on Roman and kissed him, legs wrapping around Roman's waist.

So the boy was a homo. Now it made sense why Vlad felt on edge around him.

Sneering, Vlad waited for Roman to shove the faggot away and punch him in the mouth.

Except Roman kissed back, his hands settling on Luke's ass.

What the fuck.

What the actual fuck.

When Roman pushed the boy onto the mattress and crawled on top of him, Vlad closed the live feed and stared blankly at the dark screen.

He'd known something was off when Roman had stopped fucking around, but he would've never guessed *this* after the scolding he'd received from Roman for being a little distracted by that faggot.

Goddamn hypocrite, Vlad thought darkly, a tight feeling coiling in the pit of his stomach.

Chapter 14

One month later

Rubbing his face against the coarse hair on Roman's wide chest, Luke wondered how it was possible to feel this good with a man who was the definition of Mr. Wrong.

It was kind of freaky how sexually compatible he and Roman were. It wasn't like Luke's previous sexual experiences were bad—far from it—but this was something else.

This was the sort of attraction that made him feel almost high when Roman touched him, and sex-starved when Roman didn't.

It was heady.

It was scary. It was scary how well Roman could read his body and play it like an instrument: he was bossy when Luke wanted to be owned and ordered around, he was gentle and understanding when Luke needed cuddles and snuggles, and he was deliciously cruel and scary when Luke was in the mood to pretend he didn't want it (with Roman, he always wanted it).

The scariest part was, it went both ways. Luke was just as attuned to Roman. When Roman was in a black mood, Luke found himself turning pliant and extremely submissive, letting Roman mark him and take out his frustration on him—and *getting off* on it. He got off on pleasing Roman, which was...yeah, probably pretty messed up.

The most messed up part, though, was that he couldn't even claim that he was in any way being taken advantage of or lied to.

Roman didn't pretend to be anything he wasn't. Luke didn't suddenly start thinking Roman was just a misunderstood good man. Roman wasn't a good man; Luke was perfectly aware of it, yet it didn't change how insanely attracted to him he was.

"You're evil," he mumbled into Roman's chest. "How do you turn me into such a nympho?"

He felt more than heard Roman's laugh. "It's not my fault you're a kinky little shit, *kudryashka*."

"What does that mean?" Luke muttered, not bothering to deny the kinky little shit part. "I don't know that word." It sounded like an endearment. Luke hoped it wasn't an endearment. Roman's tendency to use endearments he didn't mean wasn't endearing at all.

Roman tugged at his hair. "It means 'curly.' Or close enough."

Great. So another mock endearment.

"I'm starting to think you have a thing for my hair," Luke said.

"Whatever gave you that idea?" Roman said, running his hand through his curls.

They fell into a silence that shouldn't have been so comfortable.

"Have you ever killed anyone?" Luke murmured, trailing his fingers down Roman's muscular arm.

"I have," Roman replied.

A shiver ran up Luke's spine. Roman's answer didn't surprise him, per se—he would have been more surprised if the answer was negative—but the calmness with which Roman spoke about it was fucking scary.

Luke eyed the tattoo on Roman's arm, a single word in Russian: "*Помни.*" It meant "Remember." Luke didn't know the story behind the tattoo, but it seemed like good advice for him: he must never forget what this man was capable of.

"Do you mean personally or by giving an order?" Luke said.

"There's a difference?" Roman said, his voice very dry. "A kill is a kill, no matter whose hands do the actual deed. But to answer your question: both."

Luke traced his fingers lower, to Roman's hand. A hand that killed someone. A hand that could reduce him to a quivering, mindless creature with the slightest touch.

"Is it hard?" Luke said. "To end someone's life?"

"Sometimes," Roman said after a moment. "But most people I killed were scums so I didn't lose sleep over it. Besides, I worked for the FSB at the time, so the kills were perfectly legal." For some reason, his tone turned almost mocking at the word 'legal.'

"FSB?" Luke asked.

"The Federal Security Service," Roman clarified.

"KGB's successor?" Luke asked.

"Yes."

Luke frowned, trying to remember everything he knew about Russian military agencies. Wasn't Putin heavily involved with the FSB about ten years ago?

"Is this where you know the President from?" Luke said.

"Among other things," Roman replied before murmuring, "*Liubopytnoi Varvare…*"

Luke looked up at him. "What?"

"An old Russian proverb," Roman said, his blue eyes glinting with amusement. "Basically means the same thing as 'Curiosity killed the cat.' A very wise proverb, don't you think?"

"Are you threatening me?" Luke said with a grin.

Roman's eyes lingered on his smiling mouth for a second. "Not at the moment."

Luke folded his hands on Roman's broad chest and put his chin on top of them. "Are you, like, a Mafia boss or something?"

Throwing his head back, Roman laughed.

"What's so funny?" Luke said, shooting him an affronted look. "Are you going to deny you're a boss of organized crime? That's basically what the mafia is."

Roman still looked amused. "I don't think of myself in those terms. I make money, I'm very good at making money, and sometimes the way I make money isn't legal. The more money you have, the more powerful and influential you are and the more enemies you get. The more enemies you get, the more ruthless and careful you must be. Otherwise some people might get ideas."

Luke frowned, considering it. "I've never thought of it that way."

He looked at Roman. "Don't you get tired?" he said softly. "Isn't it lonely? What do you need so much money for, anyway?"

Roman gave him an unreadable look. He brushed his knuckles against Luke's cheek. "Are you sure you're Richard Whitford's son, baby?"

Luke felt himself redden. He wasn't sure why. It wasn't even the most ridiculous endearment Roman had ever used.

"Are you implying my father is the same?" Luke said.

Something cold and hard flickered through Roman's eyes. "In some ways, your father and I are cut from the same cloth."

"I know," Luke said. "I mean, I've suspected that he's involved in some shady dealings for a long time. I would have been a fool to be completely blind to it." Luke hesitated before meeting Roman's gaze. "What did my father do to you?"

Roman closed his eyes, looking disinterested in continuing the conversation. But, to Luke's surprise, he replied, "He thought it was acceptable to lie to me. As a result, he put me in a very sticky situation and I ended up owing a lot of favors to people I'd rather not be indebted to."

Luke's brows furrowed. "What do you mean? What did he do?"

He started thinking Roman wasn't going to answer when he did.

"I have very few principles and limits," Roman said. "But everyone who has dealings with me knows I don't break them. Your father made me inadvertently break one of them."

"Now I'm dying of curiosity," Luke said, tapping Roman's chest with the tips of his fingers.

Roman opened his eyes, a corner of his mouth twitching. "Remember what happens to curious kittens?"

"Cats," Luke corrected him.

"Kittens are baby cats," Roman said with a completely straight face.

"I'm not a baby cat," Luke said before laughing. "Also, this conversation is totally ridiculous and evil men aren't allowed to be ridiculous. You're veering off the script again."

"Maybe I'm not evil," Roman murmured, carding his fingers through Luke's hair. "Maybe I'm just misunderstood."

Luke snorted. "Right. So, what exactly did my dad do?"

All traces of amusement disappeared from Roman's face. "We had an agreement. Whitford needed safe transport for tons of illegal goods from Kyrgyzstan and Uzbekistan to several European countries." He shrugged slightly. "You can get smuggled goods in those countries for next to nothing if you know the right people. It's business, pure and simple, and as long as those goods aren't drugs, I don't care. Whitford's goods were loaded on my train. For a price, obviously."

Luke didn't like where the conversation was going. "What happened?"

Roman's lips thinned. "My trains are guarded, but usually it's just a precaution unless there's a specific cause—the trains aren't checked and are ensured safe passage through most borders. Except the train was attacked in Poland. A car exploded, four of my men died, and the whole debacle attracted too much attention to the train. It was searched and tons of cocaine were found." Roman's eyes hardened. "Cocaine certainly wasn't in the deal."

Luke winced, remembering something from his research on Roman prior to their meeting: Roman's father had died from overdosing.

"But I haven't seen even a hint of that scandal when I researched you, so you must have hushed it up?"

"Of course I did. But it wasn't easy with the deaths involved. And I don't do drug trafficking, so I didn't have the necessary connections. I ended up spending millions to hush it up and owing a lot of favors to people I'd rather not owe anything. Worse, the whole ordeal damaged my…business reputation in certain circles. In this line of work, you don't want to be known as someone who gets caught. Conveniently, your father didn't take any damage at all, even though it was his mess."

Something ugly flickered in Roman's pale eyes. "It was supposed to be a routine run, nothing dangerous. Sometimes casualties are unavoidable, but those men didn't sign up for that shit. Some of them had families. It wasn't Whitford who had to explain to a bunch of kids that their father was dead."

Luke swallowed the bile rising to his throat. He'd known his father wasn't a saint, but this…this was something else. There was knowing, and then there was knowing.

The assessing stare Roman pinned him with was unsettling. "What will you do when you inherit your father's business and everything it entails? Are you going to follow in his footsteps?"

Luke caught his lip between his teeth. "I tried not to think too much about it, to be honest." He chuckled at his own naivety. "But now…I don't think I can do what he does, what you do. I'm not—I'm not a saint or anything, I understand that sometimes you must be ruthless to succeed, but I have limits." He gave a crooked smile. "I'm not cut out for the life of a criminal mastermind. I'll make sure the company is successful by legal means. I have a pretty good head for business. Maybe Whitford Industries won't be as profitable as before, but I'm not greedy."

"As profitable as before," Roman said flatly. "You do realize what kind of money you're talking about?"

Luke grinned. "An outrageous amount I'd never be able to spend? I told you: I'm not greedy. Being a millionaire is enough for me. I don't want to constantly look over my shoulder, expecting a knife in the back. I want to live a full life, be happy, and do the things I want to do."

A derisive smile twisted Roman's lips. "Yes, you want to marry a nice man and adopt two-point-five babies."

Luke smiled. He refused to be ashamed of it. "Nope, at least four babies. I have lots of love to give. And I prefer surrogacy to adoption, though I'm open to adopting."

Roman stared at him with an odd expression on his face.

"Will I be invited to the wedding?" he said at last, his blue eyes as unreadable as ever.

A funny feeling settled in the pit of Luke's stomach.

In his fantasies, he had imagined his wedding to be a bright, fairy-tale-like event, a faceless, amazing man by his side as they said their vows, absolutely in love with each other. Having Roman somewhere in that bright, happy fantasy was incredibly jarring for some reason.

"Hmm," Luke said. "That would be a bit awkward, don't you think? Usually people don't invite their..." He hesitated, flustered. What, exactly, was Roman to him, again? "...men they have slept with in the past to their wedding."

"Men they have slept with in the past," Roman repeated, amusement flashing through his face again. His hand settled on Luke's lower back, its weight already familiar. "Are you saying you wouldn't spread your legs for me on your wedding day?"

Luke spluttered. "Of course I wouldn't! Who do you take me for?"

Roman's fingers slipped lower and touched Luke's slick, loosened hole. Luke fought the urge to squirm. He was still tender and sensitive after the sex. He glared at Roman.

Roman had the nerve to smile. "You sure you wouldn't?" he said in a conversational tone, massaging Luke's hole and teasing the oversensitive rim by slipping the tip of his finger in and out. "You would be all dolled up and pretty, maybe even wearing a white suit," Roman said, teasing his quivering entrance. "Your nice man will be waiting for you at the altar." He pushed the finger deeper, stretching him deliciously. God.

"But you'll be late," Roman said, pushing the finger in and out but avoiding Luke's prostate. "You'll be late because you'll be too busy moaning under me."

"No," Luke ground out, painfully hard despite coming twenty minutes ago. The mere idea of Roman fucking him while the man Luke loved waited for him was filthy, wrong and— "No," he said shakily, his voice cracking as Roman added another finger.

"Yes." Roman crooked his fingers a little. Luke shuddered, a moan slipping from his lips. "Yes, just like that. You're a slut for me and always will be."

"No—"

"Yes, you are," Roman said, voice clipped. He pushed his fingers against Luke's prostate, again and again. "Your nice guy will be waiting for you at the altar while you're stuffed with my cock, begging me to fuck you harder. Eventually, he'll come looking for you and he'll find out what a dirty little whore you are."

Luke groaned and bit Roman's pec. He latched onto the tiny, hard nipple and sucked greedily as his ass clenched around Roman's merciless fingers. He felt close to sobbing already, his hole sensitive and overstimulated after hours of sex, and now this…God. He moved back onto the fingers, wanting them deeper, but Roman tightened his grip in his curls, not letting him move.

"And you know the best part, kitten?" Roman said hoarsely, fucking him with three fingers now. "Even with your fiancé watching, you won't be able to stop begging me for my cock. You'll come, clinging to me and moaning *my* name." He slammed his fingers against Luke's prostate and Luke saw stars. He whimpered and came, his hole clenching around Roman's fingers.

By the time he could think again, Roman had removed his fingers and had his muscular arms crossed under his head, a picture of masculine nonchalance and cool confidence, bordering on smugness.

"I hate you," Luke said with feeling, his voice wrecked and raspy. He wasn't even sure why he felt on the verge of tears. "Kiss me," he heard himself say. "Please."

Roman eyed him for a moment, his face inscrutable, before rolling them onto their sides and capturing Luke's mouth in a soft, tender kiss. Luke melted into it, his hand burying in Roman's short hair and pulling him closer, on top of him, shivers of need rippling through him.

He whined in displeasure when Roman stopped kissing him.

"I'm leaving for Switzerland," Roman said, looking down at him. "I'll be gone for six days."

Luke felt his stomach churn. He just…he just wasn't looking forward to staring at the same four walls for another week.

Roman's thumb brushed his lip. "You will come with me."

Oh.

"Okay," he whispered, a small smile tugging at his lips.

Chapter 15

Vlad burst into Roman's office. "You can't be serious!"

Only when his boss raised his unimpressed eyes from the computer, did Vlad realize what a blunder he'd made.

"Excuse me?" Roman said.

Vlad forced himself to meet his gaze unflinchingly. "I'm sorry, Roman Danilovich, but I can't agree with your decision to take the boy to Switzerland. It's a huge security risk—he might be spotted at the airport or—"

"Do I need to remind you we'll use my private plane?" Roman said. "No one will dare check it. You will personally ensure it."

"Of course," Vlad said, swallowing his protests.

Roman's gaze turned sharp. "If you have something to say, do it."

Vlad hesitated, unsure how to bring up the subject. "You're fucking Whitford's brat."

There wasn't a flicker of surprise or shame in Roman's pale eyes. Roman's face betrayed nothing. "Yes," he said. "Your point being?"

Vlad didn't think he'd ever felt so uncomfortable in Roman's presence. "I didn't know you were...into men."

"I didn't know I was supposed to inform you of my sex life, Vlad," Roman said amicably, the look in his eyes anything but amicable.

Gulping, Vlad took a step back. "Of course not—"

"But in case you're wondering, I'm not interested in men."

Vlad frowned. "But—but what about the boy?"

Lighting a cigarette, Roman leaned back in his chair and regarded him coolly. "By the end of the year, Whitford Industries will be mine. Anything I do with Luke Whitford is done with that in mind. That's all I will say on the matter. Is that understood?"

"Yes," Vlad said, hiding his relieved smile. He had been an idiot to doubt Roman even for a moment. Of course Roman wasn't enamored with the boy. The mere idea seemed laughable now. Roman wasn't a homo.

Though, he still didn't understand why it was necessary to drag the boy to Switzerland.

"Where are we even going to keep him?" Vlad asked. "You'll be with Anastasia and—"

"He'll stay at my lake house."

Vlad blanched. "You can't be serious. What if your—"

"He'll stay at my house," Roman repeated, his tone final.

"Understood," Vlad said, reluctantly. "But I just want you to know I think it's a very bad idea. For security and other reasons."

"Noted," Roman said, returning his gaze to his computer.

Taking it for the dismissal it was, Vlad turned to leave.

"Vladislav."

He stopped, looked back at Roman, and flinched upon meeting his eyes.

Roman said softly, "If you ever snoop on me again, I might forget about the loyalty you have showed me in the past fifteen years. No one is indispensable. Not even you."

Vlad gave a curt nod and left the room as fast as he could.

As he strode down the corridor, he couldn't shake off the uneasy feeling in his gut. Roman may not be enamored with the boy, but he certainly acted fucking strange when it came to him. Ever since that English kid appeared in this house, Roman's trust in Vlad seemed to be on a downward spiral.

It was all Luke Whitford's fault.

Chapter 16

Lake Geneva was beautiful—at least the part Luke could see from the window in his bedroom. Well, technically, it was Roman's bedroom, but since Roman was usually absent for most of the day, returning only late in the evening, Luke had come to think of the room as his.

He stared wistfully at the beautiful mountains in the distance. He wasn't sure why Roman had even brought him to Switzerland. He was alone all day long.

He had to escape. He had to.

Because he was scared. Scared of what was happening to him. Scared because with each passing week, it was getting harder to explain away the way he felt around Roman. Scared of waking up tomorrow and forgetting that he had a life back home. The life he wanted to return to. He was scared of losing himself.

Scared it was too late.

There were signs of that already.

He wore Roman's clothes all the time, and he *liked* it. He had semi-permanent beard burn on his face and thighs from Roman's kisses, and he *loved* it. His body was littered in love bites and scratches and assorted bruises he couldn't stop staring at in fascination.

Roman fucked him so often and so thoroughly that Luke barely needed any prep these days. It was scary how perfectly compatible they were in bed. Luke had always loved sex, but sex had never felt this way: so addictive, so *necessary*. Never before had he felt like a man's hands fucking belonged on his body.

It creeped him out. He wasn't supposed to feel this way, not with that man.

A sound at the door made him flinch, tearing him away from his thoughts.

His heartbeat picking up, Luke turned around just as the door opened.

But it wasn't Roman.

It was a young woman. She stared at him, her mouth agape.

He stared back.

She was quite pretty, with dark hair and dark eyes that were full of bewilderment. There was something familiar about her, but he couldn't quite put his finger on it.

"Oh." She muttered in Russian, "Well, this is definitely not what I expected." She walked closer, eyeing Luke curiously.

"Hi," Luke said, tugging Roman's t-shirt down, suddenly self-conscious of his bare legs.

Who was she?

How had she entered the room? As far as Luke knew, Roman had the only key card to the room and the house was heavily guarded. "Who are you?"

Her eyebrows crept up. "Who are *you*? This is my house."

Luke's stomach tightened into an uncomfortable knot. Her house? Did Roman have a…a wife no one knew about?

Before he could formulate a reply, there was the sound of footsteps and a very pale Vlad appeared in the doorway. "Anastasia, you shouldn't be here," he told her in Russian. "Roman will be angry—he is angry already. I called him."

The woman—Anastasia, apparently—put her hands on her hips and huffed. "I'm angry, too." She pointed at Luke. "Who is he? Why is he in my brother's bedroom?"

Brother? She was Roman's sister?

Vlad pursed his lips, shooting a dark look in Luke's direction. "He's a guest," he said, taking Anastasia's arm and pulling her toward the door.

Anastasia didn't budge. "I'm not stupid, Vladik. What kind of guest would be allowed into Roman's bedroom wearing nothing but what looks like Roman's t-shirt?"

Vlad rubbed the back of his neck, looking anywhere but the woman. Luke found his face getting warmer.

Anastasia looked from Vlad to Luke before her lips formed an O. Then, a slow grin stretched her lips.

"Really? My old-fashioned, straight brother is sleeping with a guy?" Her grin disappeared as she peered into Luke's face. "A *boy*? Are you even legal?" she said in English, her accent as non-existent as Roman's. "I didn't know my brother was into jailbait, especially the male variety."

"I'm perfectly legal," Luke said, sighing. "I'm twenty-three."

"Huh," she said, her voice laced with surprise and amusement. "But you're still a lot younger than Roma. And you still lack the boobs."

"Anastasia Danilovna, you should leave now. Please." Vlad seemed on the verge of a nervous breakdown.

"Why?" Anastasia said. "Maybe I want to get acquainted with the person who has my brother ditching his family and very important wedding rehearsals every evening." She smiled brightly, walked over and offered her hand to Luke. "Anastasia Demidova, also known as Anastasia Lugova, soon-to-be Anastasia Bernard. Nice to meet you."

"Likewise," Luke said after he had somewhat recovered from his surprise. Roman was here for his sister's wedding? "I'm Luke—"

"How nice of you to find the time to drop by, Nastya," said a quiet, familiar voice.

Anastasia's smile froze. She looked like a deer in headlights.

Roman walked toward her, took his key card from her hand, and put it in his pocket. "Explain yourself," he said, very gently.

She swallowed. "I was just curious, Roma. I was curious why you never stay with your family for the night."

"Curious," Roman repeated. "And what if you came across something or someone dangerous in this house? What then?" His voice hardened when his sister said nothing. "You risked not only your own safety but the safety of our entire family. There are things you don't understand, Nastya. Things I keep you away from for a reason. Where's your bodyguard?"

"Roma—"

"Go home," Roman ground out, a muscle in his jaw pulsing. "Vlad will take you."

"Roman," Anastasia tried again, but he shook his head.

"I'll talk to you later," he said tersely. "Vlad, take her home."

This time Anastasia didn't resist when Vlad steered her out of the room, but she still waved to Luke with a smile. "Bye, Luke! It was nice to meet Roman's boy, although I didn't even know you existed!"

"Out," Roman gritted out and Anastasia left hurriedly.

When the door clicked shut, Roman swore under his breath and finally looked at Luke. The anger in his eyes faded a little, replaced with something else. "Why are you looking at me that way?"

"You have a family," Luke said, blinking. "A normal family with annoying little sisters and wedding rehearsals."

Roman walked toward him, loosening his tie. "I know, shocking, isn't it?" He gave a wry smile. "Sometimes villains have mothers and siblings, too. Not all of us are tragic orphans with abused childhoods."

Luke chuckled, although he was still trying to wrap his mind around the concept of Roman having a family. "I guess I just never imagined you as an overprotective older brother."

Roman's lips twitched again. "Don't start thinking I'm a good person, love." He put his hands on Luke's hips, looking down at him with a guarded expression. "I protect myself and mine. Simple as that."

Luke nodded. That made sense. "Your sister said she's also known as Anastasia Lugova. Does the rest of your family use that surname as well? Do they know what you do?"

"Of course they know what I do. Some of it."

Roman clearly didn't want to talk about it, his face closing off and his eyes turning colder.

Luke fidgeted, trying to ignore the insane urge to put Roman in a better mood and please him. Shit. Was that how Stockholm syndrome started?

"Some of it?" Luke said, lifting his hands to take Roman's tie off.

Roman let him, a strange expression flickering through his face. "You ask too many questions."

"You answer only a small portion of my questions, so I figure the more questions I ask, the bigger the chance to get at least some answers." Luke shrugged with a smile. "Doesn't hurt, does it?"

Roman's gaze moved to his cheek—to where Luke knew his dimple was. Roman stared at it for a moment before he leaned in and kissed it.

He *kissed* it.

Luke went still, wide-eyed and breathless, the tie slipping from his hand to the floor.

Roman stiffened. He pulled back and turned away, looking faintly displeased, and made a step toward the door.

"Are you leaving already?" Luke blurted out. Immediately he cringed, appalled and embarrassed by his silly, inappropriate clinginess. Fuck. This was worse than he had thought. This couldn't continue. He must escape, as soon as possible—before this thing could become worse.

"Already?" Roman turned back to him, his eyebrows raised slightly, the look on his face coldly speculative. He was clean-shaven that day. It made him look younger than usual. He should have looked more approachable, but it had the opposite effect. This clean-shaven man in an impeccably tailored designer suit reminded him of the cold-eyed stranger that had unnerved Luke so much during their first meeting at the restaurant. Luke had gotten used to the scruffy Roman, not this one. This one made him uneasy.

And okay, he sort of really, really liked the beard.

"Do you want me to stay?" Roman said, his face impossible to read.

Luke crossed his arms over his chest and eyed the other man. Was this all just a game for him? Everything was so calculated with Roman. Sometimes Luke felt like he was just a piece on a chess board, to move where Roman needed and to be knocked off once he had outlived his usefulness. He'd never felt so out of his depth in his life.

God, he was so sick of it.

He wanted some control. He wanted Roman to lose control for a change.

Luke took the hem of his oversized t-shirt and pulled it off in one motion. He was naked underneath it, of course. Roman didn't seem to believe in giving him more clothes than necessary.

Roman's blue eyes swept over him. Luke stood tall, refusing to be embarrassed under his scrutiny. If there was anything he was certain about, it was that Roman wanted his body. One could fake emotions, one could lie about one's thoughts, but lust wasn't something a man could fake. Roman wanted him—wanted him badly enough not to care about his gender.

"Does this mean you want me to stay?" Roman said, sounding *amused*, the bastard.

Luke shrugged and sprawled out on the bed. "I'd rather you leave," he said softly, running a hand over his own chest and sighing as it brushed his nipples. "You don't know how to take care of me, anyway."

Silence.

Luke smiled, looking at the ceiling.

"That isn't the impression I get when you beg for my cock," Roman said in a clipped tone.

"Anyone can stick a dick in a hole," Luke said, grinning. "I love being fucked, and any hard, thick cock does it for me. But you can't take care of me properly."

"What is that supposed to mean?" Roman sounded downright irritated now. Good.

Luke looked him in the eye. "I love being eaten out," he murmured. "I love when men stick their tongues in my hole and let me ride their faces."

Something flared in Roman's eyes. Something dark and formless. Was it anger? Was it disgust? Was it too much for a straight man? For a straight man, Roman was a very generous lover, not squeamish about touching Luke's cock with his hands or even with his mouth. But it seemed he drew a line at rimming another man. Not that it was entirely unexpected: many gay men didn't like eating ass, either. Too bad. There were few things Luke loved more.

"Whore," Roman said harshly.

"What?" Luke said with a cheeky smile, kind of glad Roman wasn't a perfect lover, after all. "Is that too gay for you? Then go away so I can have a nice wank. It's been a while since I wanked to my favorite fantasy. It doesn't involve you."

"And who does it involve?" There was something ugly in Roman's voice.

Luke cocked his head, wondering if it was jealousy. Probably not, but the thought tickled him. On one hand, he wanted to get back at Roman for his arrogant assumption that Luke would spread his legs for him even on the day of his wedding to the man of his dreams. On the other hand, Luke had never told his favorite fantasy to anyone. It was probably a bit creepy. But fantasies were harmless, weren't they?

Luke turned on his stomach and hugged his pillow, pressing his flushed cheek against the cool fabric.

"I'm on the beach at night," he whispered at last, closing his eyes. "I'm naked. I'm asleep on my stomach, completely vulnerable. I wake up from having someone's tongue in my hole, a rough beard prickling my buttocks. I freak out, because I don't know the man, but it kinda feels good and I don't want it to stop."

It was a bit of a lie that his fantasy didn't involve Roman: lately, the faceless stranger had started looking suspiciously like Roman. "I'm embarrassed and so ashamed of my reactions, but I can't stop moaning and pushing back against the stranger's tongue. He forces me to get on all fours and fucks me with his tongue. I want him to stop, but I also don't want him to stop—it feels so good and I want to be fucked deeper—I want more—"

Hands pulled his cheeks apart and a tongue swiped over his hole wetly. Luke whimpered, shuddering, as Roman started licking and sucking his sensitive rim. It was so much, and still not enough, and he moaned, trying to ride back against Roman's tongue. The tip of the tongue pressed into him and Luke squeezed his eyes shut, feeling Roman spread him open more and push in deeper, lick into him, wet noises and heavy breathing mixing with Luke's own whimpers.

"Please," he managed, almost sobbing, sweat trickling down his neck. Roman pulled his tongue out and circled it around Luke's hole, again and again, until Luke felt his thighs begin to shake, tears springing to his eyes. "Please, please, please—I need you—daddy—"

Only when the tongue stopped lapping at his hole had Luke realized what he'd just said. A wave of embarrassment washed over him. "I..." he started but Roman returned to licking his hole, now at a more rapid pace. Luke groaned, his body drawing tight in need. "Please—"

Roman rolled him onto his back, looming over him fully clothed but for his tie and unzipped fly. "Do you want to get fucked, baby?" he murmured, his voice hoarse and thick, eyes fixed on him hungrily. "Do you want daddy's cock?"

Luke nodded dazedly, stretching his arms up to Roman, wanting to be held and wanting to be fucked. Roman leaned down and sucked on his neck, his big hand stroking Luke's sensitive nipples while the other reached for a condom and lube.

Luke sobbed out when Roman finally pushed inside him in one powerful thrust. Fingers digging into Roman's suit, he could only pant and hold on as Roman's cock worked inside him. He felt overwhelmed, loving the textural contrast between his nudity and Roman's clothing on his hypersensitive skin.

He wasn't sure how much time passed. He couldn't see more than two feet in front of him, his eyes blurred by hot tears, his senses on overdrive as Roman continued to snap his hips into him, his thick cock stretching him wide open, taking him higher and higher. He was basically clawing at Roman's hipbones now, overwhelmed and desperate and just out of it.

"Come on, princess," Roman said into his ear, voice so low it was barely recognizable. He thrust hard against Luke's prostate. "Come for daddy."

And that was it.

With a keening sound, Luke came on Roman's fancy shirt, nails digging into Roman's muscular ass. He tried to push back against Roman, tried to meet his thrusts, but couldn't, finding himself completely weak, his heart still thundering, his cock still throbbing with the aftershocks. He let out broken gasps as he let Roman use his body to finish himself off, watching Roman's face twist with pleasure. Roman was so loud, and Luke loved it, loved the knowledge that he was the one causing those low groans and grunts, he was the one making Roman lose his self-control as Roman chased his orgasm. When Roman finally came, Luke sighed in satisfaction, feeling oddly proud and content.

Afterward, as he lay wide awake next to Roman's sleeping form, he stared at the ceiling, wondering if he was losing his mind.

Daddy.

He had called Roman daddy. Luke hadn't even known he was into that sort of thing. But then again, he'd never before been with someone as assertive and mature as Roman. He'd never felt so naturally submissive with any of his partners. He'd never before felt this constant urge to please any other man. He'd never dared to show his camp, flamboyant side to any of his sex partners.

With Roman, he felt cared for, like a pet that wanted

to be cherished by his owner. By his daddy. By his Dom.

And it was fucking insane.

He was insane.

Yes, he was a pet all right, a pet in a golden cage. Roman didn't cherish him. Roman was just using him. Roman had plans concerning him—plans he certainly wasn't sharing with Luke. Roman was the worst man he could have possibly chosen for that particular kink. Because trusting and wanting to please a man whose heart was cold and whose every action was calculated was a recipe for disaster. Luke might be a hopeless romantic and optimist, but he was neither stupid nor naive. This was bad. This was *terrible*, because this thing between him and Roman had an expiration date.

Sooner rather than later, Roman would use him against his father, and, regardless of the outcome, they would go their own separate ways. The sex was too intense already. He didn't need a kink that might leave him emotionally vulnerable on top of that.

A noise at the door startled him out of his thoughts.

Luke turned his head toward it.

The door opened slightly and Vlad's head appeared in the gap. Vlad jerked his head, looking pale and grim.

Luke frowned, staring at him.

Vlad jerked his head again.

Did he want to talk?

Glancing at the sleeping man beside him, Luke got out of the bed silently and padded toward the door. Vlad handed him a folded sheet of paper, sweat gleaming on his forehead as he kept looking nervously over Luke's shoulder at Roman.

Frowning, Luke took the note and read it.

Dear Luke,

My brother will probably kill me for this when he finds out (and he always does), but I can't in good conscience ignore your situation after I found out who you are from Vlad (he could never resist my eyes).

I'm not naive. I know my brother is far from a harmless businessman. I know he does things he doesn't tell us, his family. Most of the time, I'm fine with it. Maybe it's cowardly, but sometimes ignorance is bliss. To be totally honest, I would have preferred to remain ignorant in this case, too, because it's honestly terrifying to go against Roma. I know he loves us, but you probably noticed that he can be pretty scary. Sometimes my brother can get carried away and doesn't understand or care about hurting other people. I can't agree with him on that.

Tomorrow is my wedding day, and I want it to be a perfect day, not just for me but for everyone. I'd like to think I'm a good person. I want to have a free conscience when I say my wedding vows in front of God and people.

Yes, that's right: you'll be free tomorrow. I have managed to persuade Vlad to help you escape and make it look like you escaped with someone else's help. It was surprisingly easy, actually. For some reason, Vlad was almost eager to get rid of you.

Vlad will get you out at around 11 in the morning while Roman is gone and most of the security guards are at my wedding.

You'll have almost twelve hours to get to safety. I only ask you not to tell anyone that my brother was involved in your kidnapping. He's not a monster, you know.

Yes, he can be harsh, and he can be an overbearing ass, but he's the best big brother I could have asked for. Even when he's a dick, he usually has reasons for it. I'm not entirely sure what his plans are concerning you, but he has reasons to want revenge against your father. He probably hasn't told you, but one of the men who died on that train was Roman's childhood friend, Michail. He was a good man. My brother may not be a very good man, but he has a quality not every man possesses: he's unwaveringly loyal to those important to him, and would do anything to keep them out of harm's way.

Best of luck,
Anastasia

Luke stared at the note before slowly lifting his gaze to Vlad. The guy's paleness and nervousness made an awful amount of sense now.

Vlad nodded jerkily, grabbed Anastasia's letter from his hand, and shut the door again.

A numb feeling spreading through his chest, Luke walked back to the bed and slipped between the sheets. It took a conscious effort not to look at the man sleeping inches away from him.

He was going to be free tomorrow. After almost two months of uncertainty, he was going home.

That was all that mattered. That was all he wanted. That was what he needed.

Roman shifted in his sleep and slung a heavy arm over Luke's chest.

Luke closed his eyes and didn't dare breathe.

He was going home. He was going back to normalcy.

It was finally over.

Chapter 17

Buttoning his dress shirt up, Roman said, "Is there a reason you've been staring at me for the past ten minutes?"

Luke averted his gaze toward the window. With his knees pulled to his chest and his bare arms wrapped around them, he looked small and very young.

The morning sunlight reflected off his golden hair and colored his high cheekbones with a healthy glow. He would look like an innocent, uncorrupted angel if there hadn't been something so very sensual in the curve of his wide, plump mouth. Not for the first time, Roman thought that the boy looked more French than English.

"You're one to talk," Luke said without looking at him, a small, rather forced smile curling his lips. He was in a strange mood.

Roman eyed his profile for a moment before deciding he didn't have time to interrogate him. Luke had been particularly insatiable this morning, and Roman was already running late because of him. Anastasia, for all her nosiness, didn't deserve to be stood up by her brother on her own wedding day.

"I won't be back till late evening," Roman said, slipping into his tuxedo jacket.

"Vlad will bring you food. Tomorrow we're returning to Russia."

Catching his lip between his white teeth, Luke nodded, his gaze still averted. "Bye," he said, his arms tightening around his knees.

Roman paused by the door. "Something wrong?"

Luke shook his head, smiling crookedly. "Just sick of being stuck inside, I guess."

Roman wasn't convinced, but he really didn't have time for this. "I'll see you tonight," he said, opening the door.

"Wait!" In the blink of an eye, Luke was out of the bed and dashing toward him in a flurry of pale limbs and messy curls. He looped his arms around Roman's neck and pressed his mouth against Roman's, his lips soft, plush and desperate, as if they hadn't just spent hours having sex.

Roman chuckled, his fingers digging into Luke's round buttocks. But he kissed back, taking charge of the kiss the way Curly liked. He was rewarded with soft, needy whimpers of pleasure as the boy clung to him. Roman indulged him, although after hours of sex getting an erection was impossible even for a man with his sex drive.

But he really couldn't stay a moment longer.

He pulled back, their lips parting with a wet smack, and cleared his throat. "Let go of my shirt, kitten."

Brown eyes stared at him dazedly for a few moments before Luke practically jumped away and clasped his hands behind his back, looking flustered.

He blushed so prettily.

Roman's lips thinned at the thought. He really didn't like the effect the boy had on him.

The sooner he got rid of Luke, the better.

Without another word, he left the room, the door
locking after him.

* * *

Weddings were fucking tiresome. It didn't help that
Roman had spent the better part of the day forced to put up
with his numerous aunts' nosy inquiries about his own
marital status and when it was going to change.
Apparently, being on the wrong side of thirty and
unmarried was "tragic, just tragic." There was a reason he
didn't like spending too much time with his extensive
family. It was hard to intimidate someone into silence when
they had seen him in his nappies. Roman's mother was the
worst. She had kept nagging him throughout the evening,
wanting to know when he was finally going to follow his
younger sisters' example and settle down. She hadn't been
impressed when he had finally snapped and told her he
had more important things to do than play house with
some woman.

Roman heaved an irritated sigh at the memory and
entered his lake house. It was blessedly quiet compared to
the noisy manor he had left behind.

Vlad was waiting for him in the hall.

He knew something was wrong the moment he saw
his pale face.

"Whitford's boy is gone," Vlad said.

Roman stared at him.

"What?" he heard himself say.

"He escaped," Vlad said, shoving his hands into his pockets.

Escaped.

The word rang in his ears, refusing to penetrate his tired mind.

Then, he was moving.

He strode upstairs, toward his bedroom, Vlad trailing after him.

The lock was broken.

The room was empty. The wardrobe was wide open. There was no trace of the curly-haired boy with a dimpled smile. The bed was still unmade, the sheets rumpled and swept aside in the aftermath of the sex they'd had that morning.

"How?" Roman said, staring at the bed.

"We aren't sure. He was still here when I brought him food at eleven o'clock. Obviously I checked the security feeds, but it looks like the cameras malfunctioned around noon. I didn't find out until hours later because—well, you know why. After you told me to stop snooping on you, I didn't monitor your bedroom."

Slowly, Roman turned around.

He studied Vlad in silence.

Vlad's eyes were darting all over the room. "My guess is he had outside help. Someone must have sneaked into the house, using the wedding as a distraction."

Roman looked at the bead of sweat running down Vlad's face. "The house was still guarded by twenty-three highly-trained, professional guards, men who are supposedly the best. But, somehow, they didn't notice someone breaking in and taking my things from my bedroom. Explain that to me, Vlad."

Vlad kept swallowing convulsively. "Looks like the work of a professional. Possibly it was the British SIS. They seemed suspicious of you."

Roman hummed. "Possible," he said and watched Vlad breathe out. "But unlikely. There's a much likelier explanation, don't you think?"

"I don't understand," Vlad said.

Grabbing his throat, Roman shoved him into the wall, Vlad's head knocking against it with a thud. It looked painful. Roman didn't care. "Why?" he said, rage making him see red. "Why did you do it?"

All pretense left Vlad's face, his body sagging as though he were a rag-doll. "I…"

"Why?" Roman repeated, squeezing his throat tighter and watching him choke. Snapping a man's neck wasn't difficult. It had been years since he had been so tempted to do it.

"I did it for you," Vlad managed to croak out. "I did the same thing you did when the brat started messing with my head—I removed him out of your reach. When you calm down, you'll know I did the right thing! You've been irrational since you started fucking that little faggot! He's nothing but trouble. You can get back at Whitford some other way. You know you can."

"How dare you," Roman said. "I've been too soft with you, Vlad. Enough is enough."

Tightening his grip further, he watched Vlad's face turn gray.

When Vlad started losing consciousness, Roman dropped him to the floor like a sack of potatoes.

"You know I don't do well with betrayal," Roman said, looking down at the gasping, coughing man. "I trusted you to do your job well. I trusted you to have my back, not stab me in the back." He turned away.

"What are you going to do to me?" Vlad croaked out.

"Nothing," Roman said. "You have fifteen minutes to get of my house. I'd better not hear from you again."

"I've been loyal to you for fifteen years! Doesn't that count for something?"

Roman paused. "It does. That's the only reason you're still alive. You know I don't like it when my people start thinking they know better than me. They don't." And he stalked out of the room, anger and regret churning his insides and making his blood boil. *Goddammit, Vlad. You fucking idiot.*

Vlad was right about one thing: even without the boy, Roman could, and would, make Richard Whitford pay. The Englishman was ultimately the reason Roman had lost two men he had trusted with his life: first Michail, now Vlad.

Richard Whitford was certainly going to pay.

Soon.

Part II

Chapter 18

"Bloody hell!" Ryan yelled in frustration at the TV as Arsenal failed to score once again.

James Grayson hid his smile in Ryan's shoulder. Unlike his boyfriend, he had no love for Arsenal, so their continued failure to score was pretty amusing to him. He knew better than to say it aloud though.

James's smile faded when he caught sight of Luke sprawled on the other couch. "Sprawled" was probably the wrong word for the way his friend was seated: there was something stiff and unnatural about Luke's posture. It wasn't the first time James had noticed that about Luke ever since his return home. James couldn't quite put a finger on it. It wasn't that Luke seemed *unhappy,* per se. He didn't. There was simply something off about him. Sometimes.

James chewed on his lip. He had thought offering Luke a job at his family company would take Luke's mind off of what had happened to him. While it did seem to help—Luke was clearly happy to do what he was good at, and glad that he didn't have to depend on his father—something was still off. Luke wasn't the same.

James wasn't sure what to do about it.

He had given Luke some space, not wanting to pressure him until he was ready to talk, but it had been three weeks since Luke's return and Luke still laughed it off and evaded the topic completely.

It was as if… as if something had happened to him while he was in Russia. Something Luke didn't want to think or talk about.

James shivered and snuggled up closer to Ryan, breathing in his familiar scent.

Ryan turned his head. "Jamie?"

James pointed with his eyes toward Luke and whispered, "You see it, too, right?"

Ryan's gaze shifted to Luke.

He nodded.

"You think something happened to him while those people had him?" James said, careful to keep his voice low.

Ryan frowned. "Jamie, some criminals had him kidnapped for two months. It wasn't exactly a holiday. It's natural he seems a bit down."

"I guess," James said, but he wasn't convinced. Luke was the most positive, optimistic person he had ever known. Being locked up for two months shouldn't have affected him in such a way—if that was really all that had happened, as Luke claimed.

"I want to try talking to him again," James said.

Ryan studied him before nodding. "If it'll make you feel better," he said, kissing the corner of Jamie's mouth, then the other one. "It's not your fault, Jamie bear. You know that, right?"

James buried his face in the crook of Ryan's neck, nuzzling into him.

"Yeah," he said, without much conviction.

Logically, he knew it was unlikely he could have prevented Luke's kidnapping, but there was a part of him that kept wondering what would have happened if he had dragged his ass out of bed and insisted on accompanying Luke to Saint Petersburg. If he had been in the right state of mind, he would have done that. But he had felt so shitty without Ryan that he hadn't cared enough. He should have been a better friend. He and Luke had always had each other's back. They had very few secrets from each other—normally. That was why the fact that Luke didn't open up about his time in captivity worried him. Luke wasn't the type to brood in silence. He wasn't the type to brood, full stop.

"I'll talk to him now," James said, untangling his limbs from Ryan's.

Luke looked at him inquiringly when James sat down next to him. "All right?" he said, glancing at Ryan.

James let out a laugh. "We're not always attached at the hip, you know."

Luke snorted. "Could've fooled me. The two of you were bad enough before, but you're completely disgusting now that you're exchanging bodily fluids. You're like conjoined twins who fuck each other silly. Ugh."

Rolling his eyes, James elbowed him. "You're just jealous, mate."

"I am." Luke smiled wistfully. "You know I've always wanted to have what you and Ryan do."

"You will," James said with certainty, clasping Luke's shoulder. He didn't know a more lovable person than Luke. He was so easy to love and so ready to give love. "Someday, you'll meet a nice guy who will love you to bits and treat you the way you deserve to be treated."

Shaking his head, Luke averted his gaze. "I don't want it someday," he said. "I want it now. I need it now, Jim."

James frowned, hearing the odd note of desperation in Luke's voice. He wondered whether the last few months were to blame for that; maybe recent events had brought it home that life was short. James wasn't entirely sure it was healthy to jump into any sort of relationship so soon after a traumatic experience, but maybe that was exactly what Luke needed.

"You wanna go out tonight?" James said. "We could go to that club you like. Lots of hot blokes there."

Luke licked his lips and nodded, his fringe falling into his eyes.

James smiled. He knew Luke hated his curly hair because he thought it made him look younger, but personally, James always thought his curls were ridiculously cute and endearing.

He pulled on a curl playfully. "I almost forgot how curly you are, Curly."

And Luke just…froze.

"Mate?" James said, confused.

Luke's hand shot up to his hair. He smoothed it back self-consciously, unease flickering through his brown eyes. "Yeah," he said with a small laugh. "I guess I forgot it, too. I'll fix it."

He got to his feet, looking vaguely discomfited. "I'll pick the two of you up in a few hours, yeah?"

James's brows furrowed. "You sure you want to go out tonight?"

"Yeah, totally." Luke flashed him a smile. "I'm fine. Later, mate."

And then he was gone—in the middle of the football match they had been watching, without even saying goodbye to Ryan. Yeah, Luke was totally fine.

Later that night, as he watched Luke nurse his drink and turn down all the guys trying to strike up a conversation with him, James's concern only grew stronger. It wasn't as though Luke seemed completely uninterested in meeting someone: he made some effort, but he didn't seem to be able to muster up much enthusiasm no matter how attractive the guy was. It was like there was an invisible barrier between Luke and those men, and that was starting to freak James out. Luke was so *detached*. Luke had always been anything but. He was a sociable, affectionate person, easy to talk to, easy to strike up friendships.

"Check out the guy at the bar," James tried again with a sigh, nodding toward the man in a suit. "He's been staring at you for a while." He didn't have much hope for that one. The guy was quite a bit older than them, closer to thirty than twenty. He looked out of place in a club like that.

But, to his surprise, Luke's gaze lingered on the guy, something like interest appearing in his eyes for the first time that night. Running a hand through his tamed, barely wavy hair, Luke caught the stranger's gaze and smiled.

As the guy started making his way toward them, James nudged Luke. "Are you sure? He's a lot older."

Luke nodded, long eyelashes hiding the expression in his downcast eyes.

James studied him thoughtfully. Actually, maybe it would work. Luke had always been mentally mature for his age, looking for a serious relationship rather than meaningless hookups.

James could easily see him getting married young and having a bunch of kids—something most twenty-three-year-olds weren't ready to commit to. Maybe an older man was a better fit for Luke than guys their age.

James shifted his gaze back to the guy approaching them. For some reason, he looked familiar, but no matter how much James strained his memory, he couldn't remember where from.

"Hello, I'm Tyler," the guy said, shaking their hands.

"James," he introduced himself.

Tyler nodded politely—he seemed nice—but his dark eyes were only on Luke, hungry and a little enamored already. Taking that as his cue to leave, James picked up his drink and excused himself.

Leaning against the wall, he sipped his drink, alternating between watching Luke out of the corner of his eye and checking his phone. Ryan should be back soon—he had left to pick up his younger brother from some party almost an hour ago.

Half an hour later, James was frowning as he watched Tyler and Luke. Tyler already had a hand on Luke's thigh. Wasn't it a bit too fast?

James studied Luke's body language, looking for a clue. It was difficult. Luke sat very still, his gaze dropped, letting Tyler grope his thigh and slip his hand under Luke's shirt. Although Luke wasn't stopping Tyler, there was something off about the whole thing.

"I've never seen you here before."

The unfamiliar voice forced James to turn his attention away from Luke. "Sorry, not interested," he said distractedly, not for the first time this night.

"How do you know? You barely looked at me," the guy said playfully, leaning into him and putting a hand on James's bicep.

His annoyance flaring, James was about to put the guy in his place when an arm wrapped around his hips and pulled him back against the wide, familiar chest. James relaxed immediately.

"He barely looked at you because he's taken," Ryan said, his warm breath tickling James's ear.

"Uh. Sorry, mate," the guy said, blinking up at Ryan and staring—a pretty normal reaction, all things considered.

James chuckled, watching the guy leave reluctantly. "Maybe you should try modeling," he said, his eyes closing as Ryan started nibbling at his jaw. "At least you'd get paid for being stared at."

"I wouldn't want to make you jealous."

James laughed. "If I got jealous every time someone drooled looking at you, I'd get an ulcer. They can stare all they want. I'm the only one who gets to touch that."

"I knew you wanted me for my pretty face," Ryan said in a mock-sad voice.

James laughed again, because they both knew it couldn't be farther from the truth. Ryan had been his everything ever since they were kids. "That and your penis," he said. "I'm quite fond of your penis."

Ryan smirked against his cheek. "My penis is quite fond of you, too. Where's Luke, by the way?"

"To the right. With an older bloke in a dark suit."

"He's not there."

What?

James opened his eyes. Ryan was right. The table Luke and Tyler had been seated at was occupied by different people now.

"He was there a few minutes ago," he said, feeling a pang of worry. He looked at the dance floor but couldn't see them there, either.

"Maybe they hit it off and left together," Ryan said.

Pursing his lips, James shook his head. "It's not Luke's style. And I don't think he'd leave with a stranger after what happened. And he's been drinking. What if Tyler takes advantage of him?"

"Let's check the restrooms first," Ryan said, taking his hand and shouldering his way through the crowd. "Call him."

"He isn't answering," James said, frowning down at his phone.

"We'll find him," Ryan said, squeezing his fingers. "I'm sure he's fine. He's probably snogging the bloke somewhere."

They didn't find Luke in either of the restrooms.

James was panicking a little by the time they decided to check the alley behind the club.

Two figures were pressed tightly against the wall, the taller caging the shorter one. James recognized Tyler's suit.

At first he wasn't sure what he was seeing. His first thought was that Ryan had been right and Luke was making out with the bloke. Hell, Tyler was practically dry-humping Luke as he kissed him.

"Stop being such a cocktease," Tyler snapped, his hand slipping between them. "You know you want it." There was the sound of a struggle and then Tyler cursed. "You little bitch—"

Ryan was the first to cross the distance. He hauled Tyler off of Luke and slammed him against the wall so hard Tyler groaned in pain.

"When someone says no, it means no, you dickhead," Ryan said before punching the guy in the stomach. Tyler folded in half, whimpering. It looked painful as hell—Ryan's fists were enormous—but James didn't feel sorry for the guy in the least.

"Ryan, let him go," Luke said hoarsely, sliding down the wall and wrapping his arms around his knees. "He's a prick, but I did lead him on. I'm not entirely blameless."

"But—"

"Get him out of my sight," Luke whispered, looking at the ground. "Please."

Frowning, Ryan looked at James.

James knew there were things Luke would never talk about in front of Ryan. His boyfriend and Luke got along well enough, but they weren't really close. Luke was James's childhood friend, not Ryan's.

James eyed Luke's bowed head. "Give us a few minutes, babe? Wait for us by the car?"

Nodding, Ryan left, hauling Tyler away by the collar.

Once they were alone, James sat down next to Luke and put a hand on his shoulder.

"You okay?" he said, squeezing Luke's shoulder. "He's gone. You're safe now."

A brittle laugh left Luke's throat. "Yeah," he said, his head sagging back against the wall. "I'm safe. So bloody safe."

James's brows furrowed. "Why did you let it get so far with that prick? You looked uncomfortable when he was groping you at the table."

Luke didn't answer for a while, his eyes dull and red.

At long last, he said, "Sometimes I liked to pretend I didn't want it, so I thought...I thought maybe what I needed to stop feeling so—so itchy—was to have that guy force me to do what I don't want." Luke laughed again. It was an awful sound: empty and uncomprehending. It terrified James. Something was wrong, horribly wrong.

"But it was so different," Luke whispered, looking at the ground. "Why was it so different? I kept waiting and hoping that...Hoped I was just a pervert."

Now James was completely confused. Luke wasn't making any sense.

"He looked so much like him," Luke mumbled, something hateful, obsessed, and desperate about his expression. "Though the eyes were all wrong."

Goosebumps ran up James's spine, a sinking feeling appearing in his stomach. He knew now why Tyler had seemed so familiar to him: he looked like that Russian tycoon with cruel blue eyes—the man Luke had gone to meet before he was kidnapped. But Luke had denied Roman Demidov's involvement in his kidnapping. Luke had claimed he had no idea who his captors were or what they wanted. Why?

"You know the person responsible for kidnapping you," James stated. He didn't like the implications of it. "Why did you lie to MI6? To your dad? To all of us?"

Luke's eyes shifted to him, dark, wide, and lost. "If I told the truth, I'd have to face him again," he said, barely moving his lips. "I just want to forget it ever happened. I don't wanna see him or think about him or—" He cut himself off, pressing his knuckles to his eyes. "I wanna forget it ever happened. Please?"

His heart heavy, James pulled Luke to his chest, hugging him close. He didn't know what to say. He didn't know what to think.

"But what about Tyler?" he said, because he had to. Burying one's head in the sand could be dangerous. "What if it happens again, mate?"

"It won't," Luke said tightly, his voice ringing with conviction. "That wasn't what I came here for tonight. I wanted to meet a nice guy—not—not this. I wasn't looking for his lookalike. I hate him, I swear."

James stroked Luke's wavy hair. It had gotten long while Luke had been gone.

"He's everything I hate," Luke said.

"Okay."

"He was all wrong for me."

James said nothing, because of course a man like Roman Demidov was all wrong for such a sweetheart like Luke.

"I'm glad I'll never see him again." Luke's voice cracked.

"Okay," James said, hugging him tighter.

He pretended he didn't notice the wetness against his chest.

Chapter 19

"I like you, Luke."

Luke lifted his gaze from his plate and swept it around the restaurant before settling it on the man seated across the table. The calm, dark eyes of Dominic Bommer met his and held.

Dominic had a strong, handsome face, with fashionably cut brown hair, dark eyes, and a firm, sensual mouth. His olive skin hinted at some Mediterranean roots. He was only four years older than Luke, twenty-seven, but he had such an air of calmness, straight-forwardness, and quiet confidence about him that he seemed older.

It was James who had introduced them. He and James…they hadn't really spoken about what happened a week ago (Luke liked to pretend his breakdown in the alley had never happened), but James seemed determined to take Luke's mind off of it and had set him up with Dominic, one of his many distant cousins. Despite coming from an obscure, impoverished branch of James's family, Dominic had made quite a career by the age of twenty-seven and had earned himself a fancy office one floor up from Luke at Grayguard.

"Yeah?" Luke said, giving Dominic a lopsided smile. "Not sure why."

Dominic sipped his wine. "Are you fishing for compliments?" He had a good, sexy voice, very low-pitched and husky.

"Nope, I know I'm cute." Luke smiled wider. "It's just…From what I've heard of you from James, you don't have much respect for people who are born with a silver spoon in their mouths, which is a bit funny. You're related to a bunch of aristocrats."

Dominic chuckled but didn't deny it. "It must be the dimples. I've always had a bit of a weakness for them."

Luke could only smile back. They were flirting, weren't they? Flirting was good. James would be so pleased with him.

Dominic's face turned serious. "Look, I'm going to be blunt with you. I don't want any misunderstandings here. I want to make sure we're on the same page." He looked Luke in the eye. "I'm tired of the club scene and casual relationships. At this point I would like a husband and a couple of kids to spoil." Dominic shrugged. "I really like you, but if a serious relationship isn't what you're interested in, you'd better tell me now."

Luke swallowed, trying to fight the wave of panic. This was good, wasn't it? This was what he had been looking for. Dominic was attractive and confident without being arrogant, he was firm without being domineering, he was genuinely nice without appearing weak. He had a sexy voice and some nice muscles under that suit. He wanted kids, too. Dominic checked all the boxes. He was practically perfect. The man of his dreams.

Luke brought his glass to his lips and sipped his drink, trying to buy himself some time.

Dominic smiled, looking amused. "I'm not proposing or anything," he said, reaching across the table and taking Luke's free hand. His hand was big and warm. "I don't want you to freak out. I'm just saying I like what I see—a smile like yours doesn't lie—and I'd really like to get to know you better. Would you like to get to know me?"

It was reasonable.

Luke smiled back and nodded, trying to ignore the anxious knot in his stomach.

The rest of the date went pretty well. Dominic was easy to talk to. He was a good listener and a great conversationalist. He was funny, smart, and attractive. Luke liked him. He liked him a lot.

After the dinner, Dominic bought him flowers on the way to

Luke's flat and kissed him chastely at the end of their date, the look in his eyes fond and fascinated.

All in all, it went great.

Later that night, as Luke stared at the beautiful white roses on his nightstand, he thought that Dominic was pretty much everything he had been looking for all his life.

He fell asleep with a small smile on his lips, feeling pleased and optimistic about their next date.

He dreamed of rough, possessive hands, ice-blue eyes, and a heavy, hot body on top of him. He woke up, breathless and panting, his body tingling all over with longing and *hunger*, the likes of which he'd never felt before.

Angry tears sprang to his eyes. It wasn't fair.

He didn't want this. He wanted Dominic. He wanted to dream of Dominic, who was the epitome of everything he wanted in a man.

He wondered what Roman was doing right now.

Luke groaned in frustration. *Stop thinking about him, you idiot.* It had been a month since Vlad and Anastasia helped him escape. He doubted Roman spared him a thought, and even if Roman did, it was likely because he was annoyed by the loss of leverage against Luke's father. Or perhaps Luke had been such an insignificant pawn to him that Roman barely noticed or cared about his escape.

Luke hated how that thought made him stupidly upset. His wayward emotions proved he had done the right thing by escaping when he had. At the rate he had been going, a few more days with Roman would have turned him into a brainless, lovesick fucktoy who was happy to be locked up and used whenever his captor was in the mood.

There was another thing that was constantly at the back of his mind: it had been a month and everything was too quiet. Although Luke hadn't expected Roman to care enough to go out of his way and kidnap him again, he did expect Roman to do something to get revenge against his father. But so far, nothing had happened. The lack of reaction was a little unnerving. Even if Roman didn't care about Luke, he sure did care about making Luke's father pay. Or didn't he?

Sighing, Luke turned onto his stomach, hugged his pillow, and tried to focus his thoughts on Dominic, reminding himself that his father's problems were no longer his concern. He had made the decision. He wanted nothing to do with the mafia, drug trafficking, or the criminal world, in general.

He didn't know his father all that well to care much about him as a person, and what he had found out about him from Roman hadn't exactly endeared him to Luke. He didn't love his father, and his father certainly didn't love him. The latter had become blatantly obvious when his father had quickly lost interest in Luke when Luke had told him he didn't know anything about his kidnapper.

"You're useless," was the only thing Richard Whitford had said afterward before leaving. Luke didn't let it get to him—his father's lack of affection was nothing new—but when James offered him a job at his company, he didn't hesitate. He was done trying to be a good son. He was so done. His dad and Roman could kill each other for all he cared. Luke didn't give a shit about either of them. He was going to be happy. He was going to be happy and never look over his shoulder.

With that in mind, Luke closed his eyes and thought determinedly of Dominic's smile.

The next morning, his father's helicopter crashed in Colombia.

Chapter 20

Roman sat at his desk in his Switzerland office, skimming over the headlines of the British newspapers Anna had brought. His gaze lingered on the front page of one of them. A photograph.

"Anything interesting?" he said.

"Not really," Anna replied. "The funeral was three days ago. The British SIS does suspect the Colombian organized crime groups, but there's no proof so far."

Roman hummed. "We both know there won't be. Lopez isn't an amateur."

Anna raised her eyebrows. "Since when did you become so friendly with him? Last time I checked, you despised him."

"He has his uses," Roman said.

An amused smile graced Anna's normally serious face. "Yes, to do the dirty work for you, thinking he's following his own agenda."

Roman gave her a flat look. "Whitford did dupe him. I simply helped Lopez find out about it."

"Out of the goodness of your heart, of course."

That wasn't worth commenting on, so he didn't.

"I didn't think you'd actually have him offed," Anna said.

Roman shrugged. "Can't say I'm upset about Whitford's death, but I can't take credit for it. I left it up to Lopez's discretion. I don't have that much influence over him, anyway." He'd expected Lopez to merely rough Whitford up, not kill him. It had been a miscalculation on his part.

Perhaps that was why he hadn't felt any particular satisfaction when he'd been informed of Whitford's death.

Anna's lips twisted. "It's very rare when I agree with Lopez. The world is better off without that backstabbing asshole." Shaking her head, Anna turned to leave.

"Anya."

She stopped and looked at him inquiringly.

Roman's gaze returned to the photograph of the funeral.

"Find out who that man is," he said, pushing the newspaper across the desk so that she could see it. "Everything about him."

"Which one?" Anna asked, without batting an eye. She was used to far stranger requests. She was a former KGB agent, after all. Very little could faze her.

Roman leaned back in his seat. "The one who has an arm around Whitford's son."

She shot him a sharp look.

He met her eyes steadily.

But she didn't question his orders. She'd always been wiser than Vlad. Although she was older than Roman by fifteen years and had known him far longer than Vlad had—she had previously been Roman's father's bodyguard—Anna had never allowed herself to speak as freely as Vlad had. Roman knew she was fond of him, but she was a professional to the T.

When Anna left, Roman pulled the newspaper closer.

He stared at the photograph again.

The boy didn't look particularly heartbroken by his father's death. Given what Roman knew about Whitford, he couldn't say he was surprised.

Luke looked…different. The golden curls were straightened and tied back, his heart-shaped face pale and blank, his dark eyes serious.

Roman found his hand gripping the armrest.

He dragged his gaze away, shifting it to the tall man who had an arm around the boy's shoulders and who was whispering something into Luke's ear. It looked more than friendly.

Crushing the newspaper in his hand and throwing it into the bin, Roman pressed his lips together.

Whitford was dead. The boy was no longer relevant. Any plans Roman had had concerning the boy were no longer relevant. He didn't need any information on the man who had his hands on—

Disgusted, Roman cut off his train of thought. Perhaps Vlad had been right after all. This was unacceptable.

His phone rang.

"I've found the information you requested," Anna said when he answered. "Do you want me to forward the file?"

Sometimes he wished Anna wasn't as efficient as she was.

"Roman?" she said when he didn't reply.

"No," he said. "Just give me a short summary."

"Dominic Bommer," Anna said. "Twenty-seven, the head of the Risk Management department at Grayguard. It's the largest financial services company in the UK—"

"I know what Grayguard is," Roman cut her off. "I've met Arthur Grayson. Go on."

"All in all, he's made one hell of a career, and he seems to have managed that without making any enemies. Reportedly, he's firm in his beliefs but quite nice to deal with. He owns a charming house in Kensington and—

"Sexual orientation?" Roman said.

There was silence on the line.

At last, Anna replied, "He's not promiscuous, but he seems to be gay or bi. In one interview, he mentioned that he's looking for a serious relationship."

Roman picked up a lighter from the desk. "The nature of his relationship with Whitford's son?"

"It seems to be a recent thing," Anna said after a moment. "There have been speculations in the British media, but I can't confirm anything yet—"

"Don't bother," Roman said. "It's not important."

He hung up and put the phone on the desk, very carefully.

Then, he pulled out a cigarette from his pocket and flipped the lid of the lighter. Leaning back in his chair, he took a deep drag, and then another.

So the boy had finally found his perfect man. Good for him.

Good.

Chapter 21

One month later

Luke sat by the pool, watching the brightly illuminated house. He could hear the laughter and music even from here. It was James's twenty-third birthday, and since James was practically living with his boyfriend these days, his birthday was being celebrated at the Hardaways' this year.

Wrapping his arms around his knees, Luke smiled wanly. He was glad for his friend, glad that everything was finally going well in his life. James's happiness had been hard fought and won. It was nice to see that love this strong really existed and happily-ever-afters weren't a thing of fairy tales.

Biting his lip, Luke lifted his eyes to the moon.

He should probably go back inside. But God, he was sick of being on the receiving end of pitying and concerned looks, as if he were terminally ill. He was sick of telling everyone that he was fine. No one believed him, anyway, no matter what he said.

It wasn't as though Luke didn't understand where they all were coming from. As far as everyone was concerned, he'd been through hell in the last few months: first his kidnapping, then his father's murder barely a month after his escape. It was a lot. It truly was. But he was coping. He was all right.

Why couldn't his friends understand that their pity and excessive concern just weighed him down, reminding him of things he'd rather forget?

Like the fact that it was probably his fault that his father was dead.

Not thinking about it, not thinking about it, not thinking about it.

A movement on the terrace caught his attention. Luke smiled a little, noticing the two tall figures standing there in each other's arms. Ryan and James were kissing under the full moon, hands in each other's hair, mouths greedy and tender at the same time. They kissed like they owned each other.

It must be nice to love and feel loved.

Realizing that he was staring at them hungrily, Luke dragged his eyes away, to the smooth dark surface of the pool. Another burst of laughter came from inside the house. Luke swallowed the sudden lump in his throat. Not for the first time since his return to England, he felt like an outsider among his friends. He didn't feel like he belonged here.

But then again, he wasn't sure where he belonged anymore. If he were honest with himself, it might be one of the reasons why he'd latched onto Dominic so fast. Dominic hadn't known him *before*.

He hadn't known that Luke was normally much more cheerful and easy-going than he was now.

If Luke went quiet and didn't feel like talking, Dominic thought nothing of it. Dominic had supported him through the hectic, almost surreal weeks that followed his father's death, a silent, comforting presence by his side, no questions asked, no judgment passed.

Dominic was kind of amazing. Luke wished he were here tonight. Maybe then people would stop giving him those looks. Not to mention that Luke…might be missing Dominic? Maybe. They were not officially together yet—Dominic wasn't rushing him, considerate of his father's death—but Luke definitely missed the meaningless flirting, and the feeling of security Dominic's presence brought.

Luke wondered if this was how people began falling in love. He hoped it was. Dominic was a man he could trust not to break his heart. He was nice, confident, and refreshingly straightforward and honest. Before leaving on a work trip to Japan, he had looked Luke in the eye and told him he expected a positive answer from Luke when he returned. It was a bit arrogant but charmingly honest of him. Dominic didn't play mind games. Luke adored that about him.

Behind him, a branch cracked.

Luke stiffened, goosebumps running up his spine as the most peculiar awareness filled him.

He held his breath, his heart hammering against his ribs. *Thud-thud, thud-thud, thud-thud.*

It was silly. There was no one behind him. He was back in England. He was back home.

He couldn't be there.

A big, calloused hand wrapped around his neck.

A shudder rolled through Luke's body. It wasn't possible. He was imagining things.

This couldn't be happening.

Swallowing, he turned his head slowly.

Ice-blue eyes met his, and Luke couldn't breathe, drowning in their cold depths, like a rabbit caught in a hunter's snare.

He could scream. Ryan and James would hear him easily if he did.

"Miss me, *solnyshko*?" said a deceptively soft voice.

Luke lunged forward and slammed their lips together. Roman's hands grabbed his face, his hot lips *searing* him, his tongue invading Luke's mouth with a single-minded intensity as the scruff of Roman's beard burned Luke's skin.

God, it felt like he was drowning, like he was coming apart at the seams and the only thing holding him together was Roman's mouth. Small, broken moans left Luke's trembling, hungry lips—he'd needed this, needed this so much—his arms looping around Roman's neck, his body straining up, like a flower reaching up to the sun. Roman's big hands slid down Luke's back before squeezing Luke's cheeks and hauling him up—

Whimpering against Roman's mouth, Luke wrapped his legs around his waist and let Roman carry him…somewhere. At least he thought they were moving, but thinking was hard, thinking was bloody impossible while his entire body was shuddering with carnal and emotional need. He could only cling to Roman, hands moving greedily all over Roman's wide back, touching the muscles straining under the shirt—and God, his mouth tasted so good, he smelled so good, earthy and masculine, not at all like the expensive cologne Dominic used—

Fuck, Dominic.

Luke tore his mouth away, gasping out, "Wait—I can't."

Roman pushed him against the wall of the house, pinning him easily with just his hips. Luke swallowed a whimper as their erections ground together.

"Why not?" Roman said, his arms bracketing Luke's head, his blue eyes boring into his.

Luke licked his swollen, oversensitive lips, feeling dizzy from Roman's proximity. Thinking and talking was a challenge when all he wanted was Roman's mouth back on his.

"What are you even doing here?" Luke whispered hoarsely, trying to make his legs untangle from Roman's waist. They refused to cooperate. "Are you stalking me? That's too creepy, even for you."

"I'm in London on business," Roman said, his lips twisting. "I have better things to do than stalk you, love."

A wave of humiliation washed over him before Luke realized it wasn't really an answer. "Then what are you doing here?" he said, lifting his chin. "It's not even my house."

For a moment, Roman didn't reply. "You didn't tell anyone it was me who kidnapped you. I wanted to ask you why. That's why I'm here."

Oh.

Trying to ignore the crushing disappointment in his belly, Luke forced himself to slide his legs down. Still bracketed by Roman's arms, he took a deep breath. "Was it you?"

"Pardon?"

"Was it you who murdered my father?"

Something shifted about Roman's expression. "No," he said, looking him in the eye.

Luke breathed out, the guilt he'd carried inside of him for a month finally loosening its hold on him. He might not have loved his father, he might have barely known him, but Richard Whitford had still been his dad. It had been killing him to think that he might be partly responsible for his father's death because he hadn't told anyone about Roman's involvement in his kidnapping.

The relief he now felt was so immense that Luke found himself smiling.

"*Blyad*," Roman cursed before leaning down and sucking the skin of Luke's cheek into his mouth, where one of his dimples was. He kept on sucking. He was going to leave a love bite for sure.

"Stop," Luke managed. "I'm not—you can't."

Roman breathed into his cheek, steely fingers gripping Luke's hips. "Why not?"

"I'm—I'm sort of seeing someone." For some reason, he felt a pang of guilt. Stupid. So stupid.

His entire body protested when Roman pulled back.

The streetlight lamp wasn't bright enough for him to discern Roman's expression.

"Seeing someone?" Roman said.

Feeling oddly uneasy, Luke nodded.

It was a very small white lie, wasn't it? He and Dominic weren't together yet, but they had a tentative understanding that they would be. They were dating. Sort of.

"He's great," Luke said. "I like him a lot. So I wouldn't fool around with you even if you weren't…you. I'm not a cheater. I despise cheating."

Roman had the nerve to look amused. "I see you're still the same sentimental, foolish boy with your head stuck in the clouds."

Luke glowered at him.

Roman smoothed the wrinkle between Luke's brows with his thumb. "Is that disgruntled kitten look supposed to be intimidating?" he said, his mocking tone contradicting the hunger in his gaze. It was such an unsettling contrast: Roman spoke to him with such derision and yet looked at him as if he wanted to *consume* him.

"I loathe you," Luke said.

A corner of Roman's mouth twitched. "Is that why you're fondling me, love?"

Luke looked down and flushed, staring in betrayal at his own hands stroking Roman's chest. He jerked his hands away and balled them by his sides.

"It's just some stupid Stockholm syndrome thing," he said, blinking rapidly as angry tears welled in his eyes. What was wrong with him? He had finally met an amazing man, someone he could build a life with. Why the hell did he feel like burrowing his face in Roman's chest, clinging to him with all his limbs, and begging Roman to take him away?

"My father is dead," Luke said tightly. "Your friend was avenged. You have no reason to mess with me anymore." He met Roman's eyes and whispered, his voice raw with emotion, "So why are you doing this? You can't be that cruel."

Roman put his hands into the pockets of his trousers. "I'm not doing anything, pet," he said in a very soft tone. "I didn't come here for that. You're the one who jumped me the moment you saw me."

Glad that the darkness hid his blush, Luke crossed his arms over his chest. "It's Stockholm syndrome. I'm going to see a therapist and get cured of it."

"You don't sound very sure."

"I'm very sure," Luke said, lifting his chin. "If I wasn't sick, I'd never cheat on Dominic. I never cheat on my partners."

"Cheating implies a committed relationship," Roman said. "Has it occurred to you that you may not be committed enough to that...epitome of perfection?" He stepped closer to Luke again and leaned down until only half an inch separated their faces. His breath brushed Luke's cheek. "Maybe your body knows who it belongs to."

Luke's eyelids grew heavy and his body felt weak. "No," he managed.

"You're trembling, love, and I'm not even touching you."

Luke swallowed thickly, fighting the insane urge to lean into Roman. *I'm dating Dominic. I hate you.*

Roman's teeth grazed his jaw. "Who do you belong to, baby?"

Luke almost whimpered.

"Has he touched you?" Roman said. "He fucked you?"

Luke wished he could say yes, just to shut him up. "My father died," he whispered. "Sex was the last thing on my mind."

"Really?" Roman said, kissing Luke's cheek.

God, his lips, his beard.

"I remember differently. You've always been such a slutty little thing, always hungry for cock." He sucked on Luke's jaw, teeth sinking into the flesh.

For your cock, Luke nearly said, swallowing another moan.

"Why do you care?" he said instead, lifting his eyelids with some effort. "Why do you care if I fucked him yet or not? I was a toy to you. A pawn. But now the game is over. The king is taken down. What do you need a pawn for?"

Roman pulled back. "You're right: I don't. You're of no use to me anymore."

Luke pasted a smile on his face. "Exactly. So please, *please* don't ruin this for me. I have high hopes for my relationship with him. He's good, he's nice, and he's kind to me. We have common interests. I like him a lot." *He can give me what you can't—and won't—ever give me.*

A muscle in Roman's jaw twitched. "I'm not interested in ruining your perfect relationship. But before you marry your Mr. Nice, you might consider searching his house for stray pets."

Luke frowned. "What?"

"You're too trusting and idealistic," Roman said, eyeing him with obvious distaste. "Try living your life on the assumption that everyone is an asshole. Some people just hide it better than others."

"That's a pretty sad way to live," Luke said softly.

Roman shook his head. "Don't come crying to me when you get hurt."

Luke blinked, a funny feeling settling in his stomach. "I didn't know that was an option."

Roman lips thinned. "It isn't." He looked at Luke for a moment before saying, "Goodbye, Curly." He turned away.

Something like panic pulled at Luke's throat. "I'm not even curly anymore," he heard himself say.

Roman looked back at him. His gaze made Luke very self-conscious of his straightened hair and boring, safe clothes. He looked nothing like the barefooted curly boy in bright, flamboyant shirts Roman was used to seeing.

"Goodbye, Curly," Roman said, his tone a little different, a little tight, before disappearing into the night.

Luke sagged back against the wall and closed his eyes, trying to swallow the thick lump in his throat.

Goodbye.

Chapter 22

Luke barely slept that night, tossing and turning, and woke up the next morning feeling tired and frustrated but with angry determination coursing through his veins. He was going to erase Roman Demidov out of his mind.

Dr. Miranda Benson was a middle-aged woman with intelligent brown eyes framed by a thin pair of glasses. Her office was tastefully decorated and yet managed to look comfortable and homey. Luke felt instantly at ease when she smiled and invited him to take a seat.

For half an hour, she simply listened without interrupting him as he stumbled through his story. He told her everything. There was little point to seek a psychologist's help if one didn't intend to be honest.

Miranda's face was mildly sympathetic as Luke described his problem, but, to his disappointment and confusion, she didn't immediately agree that he had Stockholm syndrome.

"While I do agree that the isolation and the obvious power imbalance in your relationship with your kidnapper couldn't be healthy for you, you do not display the typical behavior of someone with the syndrome," she said.

"You are not making excuses for your captor. You don't think he's actually a good guy. You were able to escape. Every case is different, of course, but victims of Stockholm syndrome typically don't even want to be rescued." Her eyes held no judgment when she added softly, "As for the power imbalance in your relationship, I understand that it stemmed from your sexual preferences, didn't it?"

Luke could only stutter and blush. He'd never really discussed his sexual fantasies and kinks with anyone other than Roman; talking about them with a woman who was his mother's age was kind of embarrassing.

"Did you use safewords?" Miranda said.

Biting his lip, Luke nodded.

"Why do you think he gave you safewords instead of taking what he wants?"

Luke shrugged. "He told me he wasn't into raping anyone, and I do believe him, but he probably also wanted to make me trust him."

She smiled.

"That's what I mean, Luke: you're capable of critical thinking when it comes to your captor, you question his motives instead of trusting him without reservation. That's very good. That's healthy."

Luke cringed a little. "But I did trust him, at least in bed. He made me feel safe enough to…" His skin warmed.

Miranda didn't seem fazed at all. "To roleplay rape scenes with him?"

Luke had never felt so mortified in his life. "Um…"

The look Miranda gave him was kind and a little amused.

"Don't be embarrassed, it's nothing I haven't heard before. A lot of the time, people's fantasies lie outside the boundaries of what they believe they should feel, outside of what they think is normal. Rape fantasy or forced seduction fantasy is actually one of the most common sexual fantasies among both men and women. As long as both parties have given their consent and use safewords, there's nothing wrong with such roleplaying." She paused, regarding him calmly. "The fact that you felt safe enough with your captor to do that does indicate a degree of trust one doesn't normally feel toward one's captor, though. Can you explain why you trusted him?"

Luke shrugged, searching for words. "I—I don't know. He did scare me in the beginning, but he was also…different from his men. I've always been a pretty good judge of character. I could tell he was cool-headed enough not to resort to physical violence without good reason."

He brushed a hand through his curls. He hadn't straightened them that morning. He still wasn't sure why. Clearing his throat, Luke continued, "Until his arrival, the guards sort of used me as a punching bag when they got drunk. He put an end to that, moved me to a comfy room, gave me food and…yeah."

Miranda frowned a little. "And you started seeing him as your rescuer?"

Luke chuckled. "I'm pretty sure that was his objective. I mean, he never told me how he was going to use me, but I'm sure he wanted to manipulate me into needing him and trusting him. I figured if he was trying to make me trust him, it wasn't in his interests to hurt me in the foreseeable future.

"In a twisted sort of way, the fact that I was suspicious of him made me feel safe with him physically. And well…" He dropped his gaze and cleared his throat again, looking at his fingers. "I was so attracted to him that I had trouble thinking. It was all instinct, to be honest."

"I see," she said, without any judgment in her voice. "Have you ever entertained thoughts of being in a relationship with him?"

Luke froze.

"Of course not," he said after a moment, still looking down at his hands.

"Luke," she said. "I need you to be honest with me. Are you being entirely honest now?"

"I am being honest," he said sharply.

She said nothing.

He took a deep breath.

"Sorry," he said, wincing. "It's just…He and I…we…I always knew it wasn't going anywhere. He's everything I don't want. My father was just like him: always busy, distant, cold-hearted, and manipulative. He never had time for my mother or me. We were basically strangers to each other. I don't want that for my kids. I want love. I want a loving, attentive husband who will put me first. Someone who will take care of me." He felt immense embarrassment as soon as he said that. Now Miranda had probably guessed that he had a daddy kink on top of his other weird kinks.

"You mentioned you're dating someone," she said.

"Sort of," Luke said, relieved by the change of subject. "Dominic. He's great. I mean, we're not official yet or anything, but we've been on a few dates. We have common interests. He wants the same things as me."

"I see." She looked pensive. "Do you feel safe with him?"

Luke nodded. "Sure, he's been very supportive and attentive."

"Would you say you trust him enough to roleplay rape?"

Luke blanched. "What—" he said before coughing. "I've known him only for a month. It's a bit early. We haven't even done anything besides kissing."

Miranda nodded, her expression unreadable. "Very well. I think that's enough for today, Luke."

"What?" he said, blinking. "But—but you didn't do anything to…" *Cure me of him.*

She raised her eyebrows, looking at him.

"I have Stockholm syndrome," Luke said hoarsely. "Make it go away. Please."

Sympathy flickered through her face. "As I said, yours is not a clear-cut case of Stockholm syndrome. You kept your sense of self. You weren't delusional about his motives. You wanted to escape and you did. You're trying to move on with your personal life instead of fixating on your captor. You're convinced he's all wrong for you. You're capable of seeing his faults clearly." She smiled. "You don't need my help, Luke. You're strong."

I'm not, he thought as he left her office. *I'm really not.*

Maybe he should have told Miranda that instead of trusting the guy he'd been sort of dating, Luke kept thinking of Roman and what he had said about Dominic. He had honestly tried not to think of Roman's warning, but he couldn't. For all of Roman's flaws, he'd never outright lied to him. Why would Roman even lie about Dominic? For what purpose?

That was how Luke found himself ringing the doorbell of Dominic's house later that day, even though its owner was still in Japan.

He looked around. He hadn't been to Dominic's place before. It was a nice, picturesque house in a great neighborhood. Luke could easily imagine living here. He could easily imagine a couple of sweet kids playing in the garden.

The door swung open.

Luke blinked.

The guy—a boy, really—who stood on the other side was pretty cute. Slim, tall and leggy, he had messy, dark red hair, pale skin and large, cat-like green eyes with the longest eyelashes Luke had ever seen. He couldn't be older than eighteen, but then again, Luke knew first hand how deceiving appearances could be.

Something like recognition flickered in the depths of the redhead's eyes. "Dominic isn't home," the boy said before shutting the door in Luke's face.

Blinking, Luke thought for a moment before ringing the bell again.

"I must have confused the date of his return," he said after the door opened. He smiled brightly at the boy. "I'm Luke. I didn't know Dominic had a relative living with him."

The boy scoffed. "I'm not his relative. And I know who you are."

Luke cocked his head to the side. "Then you have me at a disadvantage, mate."

"I'm Sam," the redhead said, his green eyes flashing. "I live here."

That much was pretty obvious.

"Care to elaborate?" Luke said, still smiling faintly, but he was pretty sure he wasn't imagining the hostility coming off the boy in waves. Either the kid was naturally grumpy or he had something against Luke in particular. Luke was inclined to think it was the latter.

"No." The door slammed in Luke's face again.

Right.

Luke turned around and headed to his car.

Later that evening, when Dominic Skyped him, Luke decided to bring it up.

"I got the date mixed up and went to your house this afternoon," Luke said. "I met Sam."

Dominic's relaxed posture didn't change. He smiled, though there was some surprise on his face. "You met Sammy? He didn't mention it when I talked to him."

"Yeah," Luke said. "You never mentioned you didn't live alone."

Dominic exhaled, studying his face. "I didn't mention it because it wasn't easy to explain. Some people take it the wrong way."

Luke smiled crookedly. "I like to think I'm not just 'some people.'"

"I hope you won't be," Dominic said, his dark eyes hooded as they dropped to Luke's lips. "I like the hair, by the way. I didn't even know you were so curly."

The desire in Dominic's gaze made Luke a little uncomfortable. He told himself the discomfort would go away after he allowed Dominic more than a few chaste kisses.

Though, the fact that he didn't feel particularly guilty for kissing Roman yesterday was pretty worrying. He didn't *feel* like he had done anything wrong.

"When I first met Sam," Dominic started, returning his gaze to Luke's eyes, "he was a homeless, half-starved child. I took him home. I gave him a home." He shrugged. "That's pretty much it."

"Oh," Luke said. "That's…extremely kind."

Dominic shook his head. "Not really. You would have done the same thing if you'd seen him back then."

"You said some people took it the wrong way. Why?"

Dominic's handsome face distorted into a grimace. "Because people have their minds in the gutter. Yes, I know it looks strange. He lives with me, I'm open about my sexuality, and I'm a lot older than him. We aren't related, yet I pay for his schooling—I pay for his everything—so of course people start assuming some bullshit. Sammy's straight, and he's a *kid,* and I'm not a fucking pedophile, but some people still think I'm his sugar daddy." Dominic chuckled, like it was the most ridiculous thing he'd ever heard.

Luke didn't laugh with him.

"Are you sure you are not?" he murmured. "If I understand correctly, a sugar daddy/sugar baby relationship isn't necessarily sexual."

Dominic's smile faded. "I'm sure," he said, a hint of steel appearing in his voice. "Sam doesn't stay with me because of my money. I'm his family."

"Sorry," Luke said, trying not to show his surprise. It was the first time Dominic was anything but gentle and considerate around him. "I'm asking only because he didn't seem happy to see me. He looked…a bit threatened."

Dominic sighed, running a hand over his face. "Sammy is insecure. He thinks I'll get rid of him when I start my own family."

He looked Luke in the eye. "He's wrong. He's not going anywhere, no matter what anyone thinks."

Hint taken.

Luke forced a smile and wrapped up the conversation, claiming tiredness. He closed Skype and sagged back against his pillows, frowning deeply. He hadn't just imagined Dominic warning him in no uncertain terms that Sam's presence in his house was non-negotiable even if they were to get serious. And Roman had implied that things weren't as innocent as Dominic had made them out to be.

For God's sake.

Luke groaned, turning onto his stomach and burying his face in his pillow. Why did he trust Roman's words over Dominic's? He shouldn't draw hasty conclusions. If Dominic was protective of the homeless kid he'd given a home to, it was only admirable. Surely it said good things about his character. It showed he would be a great, caring father one day. Dominic was perfect. He was being silly doubting it. As soon as Dominic returned from Japan, which was tomorrow, Luke should say yes: that he would like to enter into a relationship with him. Delaying it was pointless.

Decision made, he closed his eyes and hoped for no more dreams.

But the dreams came.

In his dream, he was sitting cross-legged in Dominic's charming little garden. A child's giggling reached his ears. Luke grinned, watching a chubby, dark-haired toddler run toward him with outstretched arms.

Luke caught him, laughing, and lifted the adorable little boy above his head.

The toddler squealed, his blue eyes lighting up with delight.

* * *

The next day didn't start well for Luke.

He spent most of the morning in his father's office— he still couldn't think of it as his own—dealing with things that required his immediate attention and stoically ignoring the condescending and distrusting looks on his older employees' faces. It wasn't easy, considering the glaring fact that some things about the way the company was run didn't make much sense, which probably had a lot to do with the unofficial side of his father's business. That gave him a headache. Any investigation on his part could open up a whole can of worms Luke wasn't sure he was equipped to handle right now.

Finally, sick and tired of all the intricate maneuvering, Luke left the company's office in late afternoon and headed for Dominic's house again. Dominic was supposed to arrive any minute now and Luke wanted to be there when he did.

Luke would have liked to say that he just couldn't wait to see Dominic, but that wasn't true. Before committing himself to anything, he wanted to see Dominic interact with Sam.

Because, no matter what he told himself, something about the whole thing made him uneasy. Contrary to Roman's opinion on him, Luke wasn't a naive boy with his head in the clouds—not anymore. Yes, he still believed in the inherent goodness of people, and he would always be an optimist at heart, but after his fiasco of a relationship with Neville, who had turned out to be married, he would be an idiot to trust so blindly again.

When Luke got out of his car, he found Sam sitting on the porch of Dominic's house, with a cigarette between his lips.

"Hi," Luke said, walking over to the boy.

Sam stretched out his long legs in front of him, basically blocking the porch. Emerald green eyes looked at Luke sharply. "Dominic isn't home yet."

"I know," Luke said, studying the boy. "But he should be back within the next half hour."

"He'll be exhausted after the long flight," Sam said.

Luke almost laughed. The kid's blatant dislike of him was kind of hilarious. And Sam truly was a kid—he might be taller and broader in the shoulders than Luke, but there was no way he was a day older than eighteen, perhaps even younger.

"I feel like I've killed your puppy or something," Luke said mildly, smiling a little. He couldn't remember the last time anyone had disliked him so much. "What did I do to you?"

Sam took a drag from his cigarette. "I don't like pretty-faced, rich dickheads who use Dominic and lead him on. He deserves better."

Luke frowned and cocked his head. "I'm not using him."

"Please," Sam said, scoffing. "When I lived on the streets, I saw a lot of stuff, you know. I've learned to read people. I've seen the pictures of you with Dominic. You never look like you're attracted to him, like you're fond of him. There's something jaded and calculating as fuck about the way you look at him. Obviously you can't be after his money." He eyed Luke. "I can't figure out what you're after, but I don't trust you."

Luke crossed his arms over his chest, suddenly uncomfortable. "I'm not using him," he repeated, though he was aware he no longer sounded so certain. It *was* true that he'd chosen Dominic with his mind, not his heart, but was that such a bad thing? He was sick of getting his dreams crushed again and again. Clearly his heart had no clue what was good for him.

And it wasn't like he had misled Dominic at any point: he'd told Dominic he would become his boyfriend only when he was absolutely sure that was what he wanted. Until then, they were just casually dating.

"Aren't you?" Sam said, arching his dark-red eyebrows. "Are you claiming you have, like, feelings for him? Please."

Luke gave him a flat look. Who did this kid think he was? "No, I'm not saying I have any deep feelings, but I really doubt he has deep feelings for me, either. We like each other, we've been dating for a month, but with the death of my father, we've barely had time to date properly and fall in love. That's not how adult relationships work, Sam."

The boy huffed. "So you've never wanted anyone badly enough that you didn't care how long you'd known them?"

Averting his eyes, Luke rubbed the back of his neck. "Physical attraction and love aren't the same thing."

"Unless you're asexual, and I know you aren't, there can't be romantic love without physical attraction," Sam countered. "And if you really wanted him, you wouldn't string him along for a month. Nick is a catch." The kid looked *offended* on Dominic's behalf. It was oddly adorable.

Before Luke could say anything, there was the sound of a car pulling over.

Sam's entire face lit up, his green eyes sparkling — fucking *sparkling*. Luke didn't have to guess who had just arrived.

"Nick!" Sam sprang to his feet and ran toward the tall man who was getting out of the car. Sam stumbled, his long legs endearingly clumsy, reminding Luke of a baby giraffe.

Dominic took his sunglasses off and grinned, opening his arms just as Sam collided into him and hugged the older man enthusiastically.

"Okay, let me look at you," Dominic said, pulling back to look at the boy. "Have you grown another inch in a week? At this rate, you'll be taller than me soon."

"I missed you!" Sam announced, giving him another hug.

A soft smile curled Dominic's sensual lips. He hugged back, dropping a kiss on top of the boy's head. "Me, too, Sammy," he said, his voice brimming with affection.

Luke watched them with a tight feeling growing in the pit of his stomach. It wasn't jealousy. It was worse. It was disappointment and envy.

Dominic finally noticed Luke and smiled at him over Sam's shoulder.

It was a different smile from the one he'd given Sam. He was clearly pleased to see Luke and appreciated what he was seeing, but that was about it.

Luke smiled back faintly. "Hi."

Dominic let go of the boy in his arms and strode toward him. "Hey. I was planning to call you. Didn't expect you to meet me here. Not that I'm unhappy to see you." He leaned down to brush Luke's lips with his, but Luke turned his head so the kiss landed on his cheek. Dominic pulled back, frowning slightly. "All right?"

Luke wrapped his arms around his own chest. "I…I don't think I want to be your boyfriend."

A crease formed between Dominic's brows. "Can I ask why?"

Pushing his fringe out of his eyes, Luke shrugged uncomfortably. "I just…I've had my share of bad relationships. My first boyfriend turned out to be married with kids. My second boyfriend ditched me for someone kinkier when I refused to do some of the things he wanted to do. The third freaked out and dumped me when I told him I didn't really do casual and wanted a family at some point. The fourth freaked out when he found out who my father was." He gave Dominic a crooked smile. "And my father always had far more important things to do than to be a dad for me. You probably get the picture now."

Dominic's dark eyes were pensive. "You want a man completely committed to you," he said.

"I want a man who will listen and hear my thoughts, a man who will put me first in his life and take care of me," Luke said quietly, feeling a pang of regret.

"I really like you, Dominic, but it looks like you aren't that man, either."

Dominic glanced toward Sam, who was watching them with badly hidden concern. "Is this about Sammy? It's not what it looks like. He's just a child."

"He isn't a child," Luke said with a laugh. "Open your eyes. He's only about five or six years younger than me." He shook his head. "And it doesn't matter, anyway. Even if it really isn't what it looks like, he's extremely important to you. And maybe it's selfish of me, but I'm sick of getting crumbs of someone's attention and affections. Been there, done that, got the t-shirt. I think I deserve better. Everyone does. You, too." *And I'm not sure I can give you that. Maybe Sam was right, after all.*

Dominic studied him for a few moments before leaning down and kissing Luke on the cheek, beside his mouth. "I really like you, Dimples. If you change your mind, you know where to find me."

Nodding, Luke stepped away. "Thanks for everything, Nick," he said softly. "And sorry if I led you on. I didn't mean to. I really thought we could work—that I could fall in love with you." He gave Dominic a lopsided smile. "You're kind of everything I've looked for in a man. But I'm starting to see it's not enough. So, yeah, sorry if I unintentionally led you on."

Dominic chuckled, white teeth almost blinding against his olive skin. "Having a gorgeous, sweet guy on my arm wasn't exactly a hardship for me."

"Flatterer," Luke said with a laugh, kissing him on the cheek. "I've gotta go before your Sammy kills me for trying to steal his sugar daddy."

"Ha-ha, hilarious," Dominic said with a sigh.

Luke just grinned, waved at Sam, and turned away.

He headed to his car, his smile fading with every step

he took.

Yeah. Just one more failed relationship. At least this time he had ended it before anyone got hurt.

He wondered if it was time to let go of his dreams of finding the One. It wasn't that he no longer believed in love. He did. It was obvious James and Ryan had a "forever" sort of love. Ryan's eldest brother, Zach, and his boyfriend Tristan were stupidly in love, too, despite their constant bickering.

It was just…Luke was beginning to wonder if the One for *him* even existed. It was starting to feel like it was impossible to find a man who would adore him despite his sentimental personality, who would accept him with all his weird kinks and quirks, who would want to start a family with him, who would put him first when it mattered, and whom Luke would love with all his heart and body.

Maybe such a man simply didn't exist. Not for him.

Maybe he *was* a foolish boy with his head in the clouds, daydreaming while life happened around him and passed him by.

Chapter 23

He received the call the next day.

"Mr. Whitford," said an unfamiliar, accented voice. "Because of your father's death, we generously gave you extra time, but our patience is running short."

Luke's mouth went dry. "I'm afraid I don't understand."

"We paid for a shipment of two hundred units and we expect it by Saturday."

"Units of what?"

"Don't play dumb with me, kid," the man said.

"I really don't know what you're talking about."

"Kidneys."

Luke's stomach sank.

Fuck. Illegal organ trade. His father had been involved in illegal organ trafficking. Luke wasn't sure why he was even surprised anymore. "Look, whatever my father promised, I know nothing about it—"

"I don't care, kid," the guy said gruffly. "I have buyers lined up. I want my goods. If I don't get them or you go yapping to the police, I'll come after your own damn organs."

He hung up before Luke could even ask who was speaking.

Twelve hours later, Luke sat in his father's former office, his face buried in his hands, frustration, anger, and fear twisting his insides after going through his father's computer.

He was in over his head. He had hoped to put an end to Whitford Industries' shady side of business quickly and painlessly—he had no intention of following in his father's footsteps—but it was easier said than done. There were apparently *obligations* his father—and now him in his stead—must fulfill before Luke could wash his hands of this shit, and he had no idea what to do. His father's inner circle had never taken Luke seriously, and they all fucked off somewhere after his father's death, either lying low or moving on with their lives. Luke wanted to do the latter too, but first he had to sort out this mess somehow without screwing up, getting himself killed or arrested.

He wished he could just go to the authorities, but he wasn't naive enough to think the police would be able to find and arrest every single one of his father's associates. He would be dead within weeks if he did that. Not to mention that he didn't want the company's name dragged through the mud, which would inevitably happen if people found out about his father's illegal dealings.

Angry tears sprang to his eyes, and he brushed them away briskly. God, he'd never hated his dad more. It wasn't enough that he had been a shitty person and a shitty dad; he had to get himself killed and leave this mess after himself.

Two hundred kidneys by Saturday.

A harsh laugh tore out of Luke's throat. He was somehow supposed to get two hundred kidneys by Saturday or he would be dead—after what happened to his father, Luke had little doubt that these people meant business.

He didn't know what to do.

He was utterly out of his depth. What could he even do?

Unless…

His hands shaking, Luke pulled out his phone. He brought up his contacts list and scrolled through until he came to the one he needed.

Roman Demidov.

He'd found Roman's number among his father's documents a few weeks ago and saved it, hating himself a little for doing it but doing it anyway. Since then, he had tried to delete it several times; he had, really, but something always stopped him. It was a good thing he hadn't. Rationally, Roman was the only person of his acquaintance who would know what to do in this situation. It was logical to call him. Luke *wasn't* calling him because he wanted to hear Roman's voice or feel safe or something as pathetic as that.

The phone rang four times before a woman answered. She asked for Luke's name and contact information. She told him that she would pass it along to her boss, sounding like she didn't really believe Roman would call back. Luke didn't really believe it, either.

He had half-convinced himself that Roman had no intention of calling him and had likely already left England when his phone went off later that night.

Luke stared at the screen of his phone for a long moment before taking a deep breath and answering.

"What do you want?" Roman said. "I'm rather busy at the moment."

Luke turned onto his belly, trying to fight the wave of insecurity.

Why would Roman want to help him?

"I need your help."

A pause.

"What with?"

"I got a call this morning," Luke said. "Someone is very unhappy they didn't receive two hundred kidneys my father apparently owed them. And now they're…"

"Threatening you," Roman finished for him.

"Yeah," Luke said with a short laugh. "Do you, by any chance, have two hundred kidneys lying around?"

It had been a joke—and a bad one—but Roman's answer was completely serious. "I don't do any type of human trafficking."

"That's…that's surprisingly decent of you."

"I hate to disappoint, but it has nothing to do with decency. It's just more hassle than it's worth."

"You're a terrible person," Luke said without much heat. He couldn't quite muster up the disgust he should have felt at Roman's unashamed cold-heartedness. He tried not to think what that said about him.

"That's why you're calling me," Roman said, his tone very dry. "Because I'm a terrible person. Nice guys like your Bommer could never handle it."

Luke's forehead wrinkled.

Was Roman jealous?

He cleared his throat. "Anyway. That's not all. I looked through his documents, and it looks like the kidneys weren't the only shipment my father owed to people. It's…it's not looking good." Luke closed his eyes. "I'm so out of my depth," he admitted quietly. What was it about Roman that made it so easy to admit weakness? "I just wanted to move on with my life. But now I must figure out how to deal with those people, how to get them off my back."

"You want me to do it for you," Roman said. It wasn't a question.

"Yes," Luke said, trying to keep his voice firm and business-like. "I didn't tell anyone it was you who kidnapped me. You owe me, Roman. If you don't help me, I will tell MI6 it was you."

Roman laughed, sounding deeply amused. "My fluffy kitten has claws."

There was a squirmy sensation in his stomach. "Stop calling me that," Luke said, pressing his flushed cheek to his pillow. "Will you help me or not?"

Even without seeing him, he could sense Roman's smile fading.

"First off, I don't owe you anything, love," he said, his voice low. "I didn't ask you to lie to the authorities for me. And you should know better. Threatening me isn't the best way to get me to do something."

Luke's chest tightened. "Are you saying you won't help?"

"I'm saying I'll need a better incentive than that."

His mouth was suddenly very dry, his heart thudding somewhere up his throat. "What do you want?"

"Twenty percent of Whitford Industries."

Luke's eyes flew open. He let out a laugh. "You think I'm crazy? I'm not letting you anywhere near my company."

"Why not?" Amusement tinged Roman's voice again.

"I want to get rid of any illegal dealings of my company. Letting you in is very counterproductive to that."

"Sweetheart," Roman said, his voice so low and intimate that it made Luke shiver. "You do realize that about seventy percent of my business is completely legal, right?"

Luke's brows furrowed. That was news to him.

"It doesn't matter," he said. "I don't want you anywhere near my company." *Anywhere near me.* "So choose something else."

There was silence on the line, heavy and loaded.

"I'm afraid you don't have anything I'm interested in," Roman said at last. "Either agree to my price or there's no deal."

"No deal, then," Luke said, as pleasantly as he could, and hung up. He bit the inside of his cheek, trying to ignore the stupid, illogical *hurt* clawing in his chest. Of course Roman didn't give a shit about him. Of course. Roman cared only about his own gain.

His phone rang again.

Luke glared at it but picked up.

"You stubborn little—" Roman said in a low, furious hiss. "People your father had dealings with aren't to be crossed. If you don't agree to my conditions and let me deal with them, you will meet the same end as your idiot of a father."

"Is that a threat?"

"Not from me," Roman bit out.

The hurt in Luke's chest eased, warmth spreading through him. Luke told himself not to be an idiot, but he couldn't stop a smile tugging at his lips. "Careful, you almost sound like you're worried for me."

"Twenty percent," Roman said, his tone positively icy.

"No," Luke murmured, his heart beating like mad. Roman wasn't as indifferent as he tried to appear. A thrill ran through him at the realization, even though he knew it didn't change a damn thing. Even if Roman did feel *something* for him, it wouldn't go anywhere. They were a terrible fit for each other. Roman didn't want what he wanted in life. But…but it felt so good to know that he wasn't the only one, that Roman was as affected as him.

It made him feel powerful, which was kind of ironic, considering that he'd never felt so submissive with any other man. Maybe people who said that there was power in submission were right. And maybe it was cold-hearted and ruthless to use this…this mutual attraction for his benefit, but Luke was sick of having no control. As long as he didn't lose his heart in the process, it should be fine. Right?

"I need you," he said honestly. It was embarrassing how honest he was being. "I need you so much."

There was dead silence on the line.

The longer it lasted, the more self-conscious Luke felt, heat spreading over his face.

Then he heard Roman exhale. "What happened to your perfect boyfriend?"

"He was never my boyfriend," Luke said. "Turns out he's not that perfect after all. He has someone else he puts first. He can't give me what I want."

"I can't give you what you want, either," Roman said testily.

"No," Luke agreed. "But you can give me what I need."

Roman sucked in a breath. "I'm not sorting out your father's mess for a pair of dimples and a pretty mouth." His tone was harsh, but Luke wasn't fooled.

Closing his eyes, he whispered, nothing but raw honesty in his voice, "I'm scared. I need you to make it better. Make it better."

Roman swore in Russian and hung up.

Chapter 24

As the private lift took him to the penthouse, Roman wondered grimly if he was losing his mind. Was he really letting a few soft-spoken words get to him? Had he really canceled his flight to Italy for an opportunity to…to do what, exactly? He couldn't believe he was letting a twenty-three-year-old kid sway him so easily only by saying he needed him. Fucking unbelievable.

The lift stopped and the doors slid open to reveal a spacious living room.

A lone figure stood opposite the lift, leaning against the back of the couch. Luke had his arms hugging his chest, his shoulders stiff, his brown eyes wide, curls framing his heart-shaped face.

The room was eerily quiet as Roman walked toward him. Luke watched him like a prey would watch an approaching predator. It was pretty damn ironic. Roman felt like he was the one caught and pulled toward the deceivingly harmless prey.

He came to a halt a few inches away from the boy, crowding him against the back of the couch.

Luke swallowed audibly, his lips parting. Roman lifted his gaze from them to the dark eyes and cupped Luke's cheek, his thumb resting against his throat.

He felt a shudder run through the boy and felt his own body stiffen in more ways than one, the pull tugging him toward Luke and tightening its hold on him.

"You said you needed me. What for?" His voice was quiet, but it sounded harsh and sharp in the utter silence of the room.

"I…" Luke swayed toward him.

They glared at each other, their uneven breathing getting louder, then mixing, the distance between them disappearing.

With a small whimper, Luke buried his face in Roman's neck, his sharp teeth sinking into his skin. The next thing Roman knew, he had his arms around the boy as Luke sucked on his neck like a hungry baby. Roman's cock twitched. *Baby*. It reminded him of the last time they'd had sex, what Luke had called him, how much Luke had needed him. It had been heady. Fuck, Roman hadn't even *been* into that sort of thing until Luke had whispered the word 'daddy.'

"Shhh," he said, burying his fingers in the silky curls and tugging hard. Luke moaned, grinding against Roman's thigh, his hands slipping under Roman's shirt, stroking his chest as he continued to suck on his neck.

"Look at me," Roman said.

Luke sighed and lifted his head.

Christ. The way he looked…Glassy eyes, flushed cheeks, cherry pink, trembling lips… Roman wanted to lick him all over and eat him whole.

He inhaled deeply, trying to get a grip, trying to gather some semblance of self-control. It was impossible when all he wanted was to peel Luke's clothes off, sink into him, and breathe.

The sound of a zipper being undone broke the silence and then smooth fingers wrapped around Roman's engorged cock, pulling it out of his boxers.

Hissing through his teeth, Roman didn't look down, continuing to look into Luke's glazed eyes.

Luke wet his lips with his tongue, his hand squeezing Roman's erection. "I need you," he said, his voice cracking. "Please."

Groaning, Roman kissed those trembling lips, and everything else became irrelevant, everything but this boy and his sweet, obscene mouth.

When the haze of desire cleared from his mind a little, he found them already in bed and he was pushing inside Luke. The tightness around him was almost unbearable. It brought him some much needed clarity.

"Did I prep you?" he managed, locking his muscles in place. He couldn't fucking remember.

Luke laughed breathlessly, blushing. "A little. I'm good. No condom, though."

"*Mat tvoiu*," Roman swore and forced himself to pull out.

"Wait," Luke said. He looked up at Roman, his gaze heavy-lidded. "Can I trust you?"

The question felt loaded, the answer more complicated than he wanted it to be.

Breathing hard, Roman considered his answer, gathering all his willpower not to throw the boy's legs over his shoulders and pound into him like a savage. He wanted it—wanted to fuck him without a rubber, wanted to come inside him and fill him up until the boy was dripping and then some. But Luke wasn't asking just about sex.

"You can," he said, holding Luke's gaze.

Luke shuddered. His legs, sprawled open with Roman between them, spread even wider, and he hooked his ankles around Roman's hips, pulling him closer. "Okay, then. I've never done this without a condom before, but I want to. Don't stop—Oh God."

Gritting his teeth, Roman pushed in a little deeper, the tight heat enveloping him, and goddammit, it felt...Luke made a whimpering sound, dark eyes glazed, cheeks pink and lips swollen and slack as he panted. Christ, the boy looked completely gone already.

"Good?" Roman said, and Luke nodded dazedly, his cock lying heavy and full against his belly, flushed dark and wet at the tip. Roman wanted to touch it but knew it would be too much right now: the boy looked overstimulated already.

He watched himself disappear in Luke's hole, fascinated by the sight of his thick cock splitting him open. Holding Luke steady by the hips, he slid in all the way, slick heat all around him and so tight it was driving him insane.

Luke grabbed at a fistful of duvet. "God, God, oh God." He looked totally wrecked, his teeth chewing at his bottom lip, his dark eyes watering.

"More," he choked out, and Roman drew his hips back a little before thrusting back in, dragging his cock against Luke's prostate. Luke whined, arching under him. Roman did it again, his eyes fixed on Luke's face, which was sweaty, wild, completely dazed, and beautiful. The boy looked *drugged*, like he was high off it, off the feeling of Roman's cock stretching him open, rocking back and forth, driving in deep.

Roman stroked Luke's thighs, holding them apart, thumbs pressed into the tender skin on the inside. He started thrusting harder, low grunts leaving his throat. Luke gazed up at him with those wide eyes, his golden curls damp and dark with sweat plastered to his forehead, his cock leaking pre-come. He moaned brokenly.

"I'm—fuck, I'm gonna—" he croaked out, and Roman didn't even have time to process it before Luke shuddered and came untouched onto his chest, cock pulsing and twitching.

Roman could only stare at him. It wasn't the first time Luke had come untouched, but it was the first time he came untouched thirty seconds into sex.

Groaning, Luke covered his face with his hands. "Oh my God, this is so mortifying," he mumbled before peeking between his fingers at Roman and starting to giggle madly.

A sudden wave of affection for this ridiculous boy washed over him.

"Sorry, I swear I'm not actually thirteen," Luke managed between bouts of giggles.

Roman locked his jaw, because Luke's laughter caused his inner walls to squeeze around Roman's cock, which wasn't helping his self-control at all. Goddammit. How could this boy look so incredibly endearing and make him want to fuck him up so badly?

Probably taking his silence for something it wasn't, Luke stopped laughing. "Are you actually annoyed?" he said, a note of uncertainty appearing in his voice.

"Don't be silly," Roman said, breathing deeply through his gritted teeth. "It's fine."

"Really?"

Roman rubbed Luke's come into his soft belly in circling motions. "You look beautiful when you're desperate for it," he said, staring hungrily at the flushed young man under him. "You were perfect, kitten." Roman blamed his dick for all this sentimental nonsense coming out of his mouth. "You're perfect," he said, stroking Luke's cock.

Luke's eyes glazed over, his cock starting to harden again. "It's just been so long since we did this."

Roman pulled out slowly and pushed back in. "Good," he said and set a steady rhythm, watching Luke's expression turn dreamy and far away. "You didn't let anyone touch you. Such a good boy."

Luke smiled at the praise, his eyelids heavy as he moved to meet Roman's thrusts. "Wanted only you. I missed y—this."

The words jolted through his body. Roman knew this was a dangerous road to go down, but he didn't know how to stop this train-wreck.

Scooping Luke into his arms, he rolled onto his back. "Ride me, *kotyonok*," he said, hands running over Luke's chest, tweaking the pink nipples.

Luke nodded eagerly, looking down at him through hooded eyes, his curls in disarray, his expression completely open and *lovestruck*.

Roman stared back at him, hoping he didn't have a similar look on his face. Shit, the way this boy affected him was ridiculous. He couldn't drag his gaze away as Luke rode him languidly, his dark eyes becoming more unfocused as Roman murmured praises about how well he was doing, how perfect Luke felt around him, how perfect he was.

Before long, Luke seemed completely *zoned out*, just sitting on Roman's cock and swaying dazedly. Jesus.

Roman sat up and, pulling Luke tightly to his chest, bucked his hips up, driving his aching cock hard inside the boy's pliant body, causing Luke to moan against the side of Roman's neck and cling to him.

It went on for a long while, with Roman fucking the boneless body in his arms. At some point, Luke groaned and sank his teeth into his neck, coming all over Roman's chest and stomach, and Roman finally let go, his orgasm ripping through him with full-body shudders as he spilled inside Luke.

When his head cleared a little, Roman found that he had the boy cradled against his chest, his fingers carding through the moist curls. Luke was nuzzling into his collarbone, all but purring. He really was such a kitten.

"Why is it always so good with you?" Luke mumbled, still sounding half out of it. "Like, I feel like I'm in heaven when I give all control to you. It feels so, so good. Wanna feel this forever."

Roman reminded himself that Luke didn't know what he was saying: he was still riding high on the afterglow.

Luke sighed. "Dr. Benson's wrong," he muttered into Roman's neck. "I totally have Stockholm syndrome. I need help."

"Then what do I have?" Roman said. He regretted it as soon as the words left his mouth.

Luke lifted his head and looked at him unblinkingly, his plump lips forming an O.

Resisting the urge to avert his gaze, Roman wondered if the boy's sentimental foolishness was contagious.

Luke bit his lip but failed to suppress his smile. "Well, I've been told I'm very likable," he said, as if sharing a huge secret, a dimple appearing in his cheek.

Roman wanted to kiss it.

"This is not amusing," he said tersely. "This is… an inconvenience."

"Inconvenience," Luke repeated, eyeing him curiously. "You mean your…attraction to me?"

Attraction.

The word didn't feel adequate. Roman nodded nevertheless. He saw little point in denying the attraction; it would be pointless, considering where his cock still was.

Luke pulled a funny face. "I'll have you know this attraction to you is extremely inconvenient for me, too," he said and looked at Roman expectantly—*trustingly*. "What are we going to do about it, then?"

Goddammit, was the boy even aware of the way he looked at him? Roman would like to say that Luke's lovesick looks bothered him or amused him, but that would be a lie.

The truth was, he didn't mind.

The truth was, he fucking liked it.

He liked it.

The truth was, he wanted his boy to keep looking at him that way—*his boy*. Jesus Christ. His own possessiveness made him cringe.

"You used to make me really nervous when you got this look on your face," Luke said amicably.

Roman slid his hands down the graceful curve of Luke's back and settled them on his cheeks. "Are you saying I don't make you nervous anymore?" Few people in the world could claim such a thing.

Luke smiled crookedly. "You do. Just in a different way." He seemed to hesitate before admitting, embarrassment coloring his voice, "You aren't blind. It would be pretty pointless to deny I get off on pleasing you. I get anxious if I don't." Luke rubbed the back of his neck with his hand. "It's pretty inconvenient. Can't wait to get cured of this."

"Cured," Roman repeated.

"Of my Stockholm syndrome," Luke clarified serenely.

Roman felt a hot, irrational spike of displeasure. "Good luck with that," he said, lifting Luke and depositing him on the bed before getting to his feet. He reached for his boxers on the floor and slipped into them.

"You're leaving already?"

Roman looked back.

There was an unhappy wrinkle between Luke's brows, the corners of his lips turned downward.

"What do you want me here for?" Roman said. "I'm sure your therapist would tell you that spreading your legs for your former captor isn't conducive to getting cured."

A rosy blush appeared on Luke's cheekbones. He chewed on his lip. "What about the threats I've been getting? I really need your help."

Roman knew the sort of people Whitford had dealings with. They would eat this baby-faced young man alive. He wished he could say he didn't care. He did. There was no rational reason for that, no logical motive. He just did. No matter what he told himself, he couldn't see this soft-spoken, head-in-the-clouds, sentimental boy as anything but *his*. It was frustrating, because Roman didn't want to want any claim of that sort.

"I'll deal with it," he said curtly.

Luke beamed at him, his eyes bright, dimples in full force.

For fuck's sake.

"Now?" Luke said hopefully, eagerness and longing written all over his face. "I have everything on my laptop here." *Don't go,* Luke's eyes said. *Don't go,* his body said.

It would have been cringe-inducing if Roman didn't feel the same irresistible pull toward him. Only, unlike Luke, he couldn't conveniently claim being affected by any sort of syndrome.

"Get the laptop," he bit off and sat down on the bed.

When Luke brought his laptop to the bed and snuggled up against him, Roman didn't push him away.

He should have. The boy was a menace.

Chapter 25

His therapist's unfaltering gaze on him was pretty unnerving.

Luke squirmed and regretted it immediately. He was still feeling last night's activities.

"Why are you here, Luke?" Miranda said at last. "What do you hope to achieve by seeing me?"

"I…" He licked his lips. "I told you already. I want you to help me get cured of this—of my Stockholm syndrome. I want to get him out of my head."

She cocked her head, regarding him over the rim of her glasses. "And yet you're continuing sexual relations with that man."

Luke bit his knuckle, avoiding her eyes. "You'll fix me eventually, so what difference does it make?"

"Luke," Miranda said calmly but with an undertone of reproach. "I'm not a magician. I can't help you if you don't make an effort yourself. Your attitude isn't that different of a woman who chooses to have unprotected sex only because she can take a 'morning-after' pill. It is, in fact, worse, because there's no such pill for you."

Luke dropped his face into his hands, his shoulders slumping.

"I know," he said. "It's just…it's hard." Sighing, he lifted his head and looked at his therapist miserably. "I feel so good with him. So, so good."

Miranda didn't look particularly surprised.

"What do you mean by 'good?' Could you elaborate?"

Luke thought of the way he felt this morning when he woke up in Roman's arms.

"Giddy," he said. "Safe," he said quieter, feeling like a freak. Roman was the last person he should be feeling safe with. "I need help," he said, desperation sneaking into his voice.

"Any kind of BDSM relationship requires a high level of trust in your partner," Miranda said. "Trust of your safety, trust of taking care of you, trust to read you correctly and give you what you need. It can create a deep bond between two people that goes beyond sex."

"But we aren't—we don't always…do it," Luke said, his face aflame. "I'm not even into pain. I'm not into whips and things like that. I just like being…" He trailed off, unsure, because the first word that he sprang to his mind was *his*.

"Taken care of?" Miranda suggested. "Like you belong to someone?"

Luke nodded hesitantly. She wasn't wrong, but he didn't really want to talk about it. Truth be told, Roman was the only person he felt comfortable enough to discuss—and do—those things with.

"A BDSM relationship doesn't necessarily contain bondage or sadomasochism," she said, but as if sensing his reluctance to talk about it, she changed the subject. "Would you say you feel less attached to him now that you're free?"

Luke thought of this morning—of how reluctant he had been to move from Roman's wide, comfy chest when it was time to get up. Of how he couldn't stop sneaking kisses while he made breakfast for them. Of how he let Roman suck a bruise on his neck in the underground parking garage before they got into their respective cars. Of how he had been obsessively checking his phone all day, barely able to focus on work.

Luke cleared his throat. "Not really."

He left the therapist's office with more questions than answers.

Halfway to his flat, he noticed something that finally distracted him from the questions in his mind and the silent phone in his pocket.

A black minivan was following his car. He was pretty sure he'd seen that car parked by Miranda's office when he left it.

His heart in his throat, Luke glanced at the rear-view mirror again before pulling out his phone and hovering his thumb over the number Roman had programmed into his phone this morning.

"In case of an emergency," Roman had told him, his expression unreadable. He had given Luke no reason to believe last night wasn't a one off. Luke had wanted to ask whether Roman was coming tonight or not, but he hadn't wanted to seem clingy. He didn't want to *be* clingy. It was bad enough that he had been forced to ask for Roman's help. It was bad enough that last night he had been gagging for it so badly that he had behaved like a teenager getting his first taste of cock.

But this surely counted as an emergency, right?

It was completely reasonable to call Roman if a suspicious car was following him home, especially in the light of recent events, wasn't it?

"Demidov," Roman said when he answered.

"Someone's following my car," Luke said without any preamble, trying to ignore the silly butterflies in his stomach that appeared at the sound of Roman's voice. *He's all wrong for you*, he reminded himself. *Wrong, wrong, wrong. He's no Prince Charming. If anything, he's the villain.*

There was silence on the line for a moment.

Then, Roman said, "Drive home as usual. I'll take care of it."

He hung up.

Luke let out the breath he'd been holding, warmth spreading down his chest and curling in his stomach. "Don't be stupid, Luke," he whispered. *I'll take care of it* wasn't an equivalent of *I'll take care of you*. Feeling tingly and warm on the inside every time Roman was there for him when he needed him was silly. It didn't mean anything. It couldn't mean anything with a man like Roman Demidov.

Not to mention that Luke shouldn't want it to mean anything—not with Roman.

"Stupid," he muttered and forced himself to focus on the minivan in the rear-view mirror. He wondered if he should be freaking out that after telling Roman about the car he felt completely calm now. He wouldn't want to become reliant on Roman to always be there to swoop in and save the day. He wasn't a bloody damsel in distress and Roman wasn't his knight in shining armor. Maybe he should hire a few bodyguards, at least for the time being. Maybe.

The minivan followed him all the way home.

Luke parked in the underground garage and hesitated. He couldn't see Roman anywhere. The minivan stopped, too. The garage was eerily quiet.

Swallowing, Luke got out of his car and headed for the lift. His footsteps echoed in the dimly lit garage.

Why weren't there any people? Where was the nosy Mrs. Bale from the tenth floor when Luke actually wouldn't mind talking to her?

There was the sound of multiple footsteps behind him.

Luke started walking faster, a heavy lump of disappointment growing inside him. Idiot. He had been an idiot to trust Roman.

"If you scream, you're dead," a harsh voice said as someone pressed a gun against Luke's back.

Luke didn't scream. He didn't resist when hands grabbed his arms and pushed him toward the minivan — there was little point. He was shoved inside so roughly he stumbled and would have face-planted if a pair of hands didn't stop his fall.

A very familiar pair of hands.

Luke gaped at Roman, confusion and anger warring inside him. "What the fuck?"

The minivan's door closed, leaving them alone in the semidarkness.

Roman let go of his arms and leaned back against the seat, leveling him with a distinctly unimpressed look.

"I could ask you the same thing. It's the second time my men were able to kidnap you without any effort whatsoever, you careless little idiot. Where are your bodyguards?"

Luke flopped into the opposite seat and crossed his arms. "I don't have them. And I'd appreciate it if you stop calling me an idiot and explain to me why you kidnapped me—again."

"It was a test and you failed it." A muscle pulsed in Roman's jaw. "I've looked over the files that you gave me. Do you have any idea how dangerous some of those people are?"

The heavy lump of disappointment loosened and disappeared. Luke hid a smile behind his hand. "You're worried about me."

Roman's blue eyes flashed.

Grabbing Luke's arm, he yanked him toward him and gripped his throat. "Don't you understand the meaning of the word 'dangerous,' you reckless, foolish boy? If those people get their hands on you, you will wish you were dead."

Luke wet his dry lips with his tongue. "But I noticed the minivan, didn't I? And I called you."

Roman's lips thinned.

"You know I'm right," Luke said, meeting his eyes. "If they hadn't been your own people, you would have come to my help."

If anything, Roman looked even more pissed off. "Stop looking at me that way," he grated out, his expression managing to be stormy and hungry at the same time.

"What way?"

"Like I'm a goddamn hero," Roman gritted out before shoving his tongue down Luke's throat.

Luke sighed happily and stopped thinking.

Minutes later, when Roman pulled back and he could think again, Luke found himself curled in the older man's lap, his hand under Roman's shirt, his lips well-kissed and swollen. He smiled at Roman, not particularly bothered by the grim, pinched look on Roman's face.

"I'll give you a few bodyguards and you'll take them with you wherever you go," Roman said, his hands holding Luke's waist, thumbs stroking his belly and causing delicious goosebumps run across his skin. "It won't be permanent," Roman said. "Only until I'm done dealing with the mess Whitford left."

And then what? Luke nearly asked before berating himself. Of course he knew what would come next: Roman would leave.

Dropping his gaze, Luke nodded.

"Okay, if that's all…" he said, letting his hand drag down Roman's warm, muscular chest. He looked through his eyelashes at Roman and licked his lips. "Are you coming up with me?"

Roman stared at him, his jaw set. He looked so pissed off Luke thought he would say "no" for sure.

He was wrong.

Chapter 26

Two months later

"Nice," the woman said, looking around the spacious suite appreciatively.

Roman shrugged, casting a disinterested glance over the room. Paris, Milan, London, now New York…There came a point when all the luxury hotels started looking the same.

Unhurriedly, he took his tie off.

"Let me," she said with a flirtatious smile, pushing his hand away and starting to unbutton his shirt.

Roman let his eyes follow the curves of her half-naked body, trying to muster up interest in it. He should have been more than interested. It had been a while since he'd had a woman. Almost half a year. For him it was unheard of. For him it was unheard of to stay monogamous for a week, let alone half a year. The most peculiar thing was, no one forced him to stay monogamous. Luke knew better than to request it aloud, though his eyes told a different story.

The boy had been increasingly affectionate and needy, greeting him with a sunny smile whenever Roman returned to London between his trips.

This had been the last trip he'd undertaken on Luke's behalf. It had taken him almost two months to deal with the mess Whitford had left after himself, but now it was over. He had no reason to keep returning to London.

"Am I boring you?" the woman said with a playful pout, brushing her fingers against his crotch through his trousers. Her American accent seemed strange after months of hearing a British one.

"I'm not a teenager, sweetheart," Roman said. "I'm not going to get worked up just from seeing a half-naked woman, no matter how pretty she is." He determinedly didn't think about the fact that he had no problem getting hard just from looking at the curve of a certain English boy's lips.

A sense of unease settled in the pit of his stomach. Irritated, Roman dragged her close and kissed her roughly, making a conscious effort to focus on the softness of her lips and breasts. But the shape of her lips was all wrong, her mouth wasn't sweet enough, and her hair was too straight and not soft enough—

Roman broke the kiss and turned his back to her. "I've changed my mind. Get out." His words were clipped and tight with anger, and he wasn't surprised when she left without saying a word.

As soon as the door clicked shut after her, Roman shrugged his shirt off, balled it in his fist and tossed it across the room. Goddammit.

So much for his attempt to prove he wasn't fixated on Luke Whitford.

He was fixated, all right.

More than fixated.

Heaving a sigh, Roman sat on the bed and ran a hand over his face.

He was thirty-two years old. Not exactly an age to wallow in denial. Perhaps it was time to call a spade a spade, no matter how inconvenient for him the truth was.

And the truth was, he wanted only his curly-haired English boy.

He wanted to own him.

He wanted to keep him.

Hell, he would keep him in his pocket if he could, to have 24/7 access to him. He wanted to be able to bury his face in Luke's soft curls and suck marks into his skin whenever he wished. He wanted to have the right to do it.

The question was whether he should do anything about it.

Roman wasn't used to denying himself anything, alcohol and drugs being the only exceptions. But wanting Luke...it wasn't a simple matter of taking what he wanted. It wasn't even Luke's gender that made him hesitate: Roman was long past that point. He didn't care that Luke had a cock instead of a vagina. He was pretty much in love with the boy's nice little body and wouldn't change a thing about it.

No, the problem was more complicated than Luke's sex. The boy had been hurt in the past. He was too damn vulnerable. Luke wanted the type of commitment that would send most men running in the opposite direction. Luke also had an unsettling knack for making him want to be a better man than he was and to protect him from every hurt and harm.

A prime example of it was when Luke had asked him whether Roman was the one to kill his father and Roman answered no.

While technically he hadn't lied, it wasn't the full truth: he'd certainly played a part in Whitford's death, however indirect. But he had omitted it, knowing the silly boy would be crippled with guilt, regardless of the fact that his father wasn't worth it.

All in all, Luke Whitford would needlessly complicate his life. Getting involved with him would be irrational, impractical, and dangerous. Roman would have to make compromises and sacrifices he wouldn't make otherwise.

Sighing, Roman pinched the bridge of his nose.

He had to make the decision.

Chapter 27

Anna wasn't amused. Granted, she wasn't easily amused, but the way her boss had been behaving for the past two months made her decidedly unamused. For the past two months? Perhaps it would be more correct to say the past half a year, ever since Roman kidnapped Whitford's son and made him his pet—at least that was how Vlad had reported it to her while she was busy sealing a multi-million deal on Roman's behalf in France.

At the time, Anna had been skeptical and didn't take Vlad's words seriously: Roman had never shown any interest in men, so she was convinced it was part of some elaborate scheme to make Richard Whitford pay. By the time she had returned from France, Anna found the boy already gone, Vlad given the boot, and Roman restless in a way she'd never seen before.

There had been a certain tension about Roman, something tightly coiled around his shoulders in the following weeks. The most obvious reason she could think of at the time was that Roman had stopped sleeping around, and for Roman, it was nearly unheard of. Even Whitford's death hadn't seemed to appease him. If anything, Roman looked more on edge after that.

Anna started suspecting the real reason for Roman's strange mood when he had asked her to find out everything about Dominic Bommer. With Whitford dead, there could have been only one reason for Roman's interest: the beautiful young man in Dominic's half-embrace. She could almost see the appeal: the boy had very fine facial features and a mouth to die for.

Except Anna would have never thought that was Roman's type—or anything with a penis, for that matter. But even then, she hadn't suspected the extent to which Luke Whitford affected her normally unflappable, cool-headed boss.

Roman's impulsive, unscheduled trip to London had been the first clue. When he disappeared into the night after dismissing his bodyguards, Anna hadn't been amused in the least—with Vlad fired, security had been added to the long list of her responsibilities, and Anna didn't appreciate it when Roman didn't let her do her fucking job. Thankfully, Roman had returned to his hotel room a few hours later, safe and sound. But when she let herself into Roman's room to let him know how displeased she was, she found him on the floor, gripping a bottle of vodka in his hand and staring at it hungrily.

The sight gave her pause. Roman didn't drink. Not anymore.

It was common knowledge that Roman's father had died from overdosing when Roman was seventeen, but few people knew he had actually been poisoned with drugs. Danil Demidov had been a harsh, unsympathetic businessman but an excellent husband and father. He and Roman had been very close, and Danil's death had hit Roman hard.

Anna knew Roman had killed the man responsible for his father's death himself. It went only downhill from there. Roman had started drinking. It went on for months until eventually he was hospitalized with severe alcohol poisoning. When Anna arrived at the hospital, she found Roman's mother clinging to him, crying and begging him not to do it to her and to the girls.

Who's going to protect us if you're gone, too, Roma? she had said at last when her son had remained deaf to her pleas.

To Anna's knowledge, Roman had never touched alcohol again. But he did keep it at hand. When Anna had asked him a few years ago why he kept alcohol if he never drank it, Roman told her he liked to test himself.

That was why when Anna had seen Roman staring at the bottle of vodka with a scary sort of intensity, his jaw clenched tight, an alarm rang in her mind.

When a few days later he canceled his flight to Italy and dismissed his bodyguards once again, Anna was more than a little annoyed.

However, when Roman called her the next day, she noticed the change in him immediately: he sounded more relaxed, the tight snappishness in his voice gone. When he informed her of his whereabouts so she could send his bodyguards, she almost wasn't surprised to learn that he was at Luke Whitford's penthouse. Almost.

But even then she hadn't known how much everything would change.

In the following weeks, Roman had made her reorganize his schedule, delegating most of his responsibilities and leaving London only for the most important business meetings.

As soon as the meeting was over, Roman would be on his plane, flying back to London. He was also spending a good chunk of his valuable time helping Luke Whitford sort out the mess his father had left.

Anna watched all of that with a mixture of surprise and disbelief. In all the years she had known Roman, she had never seen him so...fixated on anyone. She called it fixation for lack of a better word. Granted, she hadn't seen Roman interact with Luke Whitford, but since Roman didn't allow anyone to get close to him, preferring to keep even his family at arm's length for their own safety, she concluded it could only be sex.

So she had waited patiently for Roman to get over his strange obsession with Whitford's boy, and with every passing week that it didn't happen, her confusion grew stronger.

But Anna knew better than to question Roman's decisions aloud. Of course, it didn't mean she couldn't try to interrogate him.

"So," Anna said as soon as Roman emerged out of the shower. He had just arrived from the airport fresh from New York City. If the pattern established in the last two months held true, he would finish changing and leave to see his curly-haired boy.

Roman let his towel drop and opened the wardrobe. "Yes, Anna?"

She took a moment to admire his physique, musing whether or not her attachment to Roman would have been less sisterly if she were fifteen years younger than she was.

"For how much longer are we going to be based in England?" Anna's tone was carefully casual. "We've barely left England for two months."

At her question, Roman's hands paused. Pale eyes scrutinized her.

She refused to be intimidated. She was a former KGB agent. She wasn't easily intimidated.

Pressing his lips together, Roman pulled on a pair of trousers. "Actually, I want you to start looking for a large building in London. Good, secure location is the priority. The price doesn't matter."

She sucked in a sharp breath. "You mean…"

"Yes," Roman said. "I'm moving the main office from Geneva to London."

Anna could only stare at him in silence.

Moving the headquarters from a tax haven like Switzerland to the UK wasn't the most practical decision. To put it mildly.

She opened her mouth and closed it without saying a word.

Roman let out a sigh. "You have two minutes to voice your objections," he said, shrugging into a fresh shirt and starting to button it up.

"As your employee, it's not my place to object," Anna said before letting a slow grin stretch her lips. "But as your old friend, let's just say I never thought I'd see the day you'd let some baby-faced English kid plait ropes out of you. Smitten is a good look on you."

Roman leveled her with a withering look.

Anna flinched but held his gaze, her lips twitching.

Grabbing his keys, he said, "Focus on doing your job, Anya."

She watched him leave, smiling faintly. She had no idea how Whitford's kid had accomplished that, but she was glad. Roman worked too much.

Anna was the same way, but there was one significant difference between her and Roman: she always had a home to return to; Roman didn't.

Perhaps that was about to change.

Chapter 28

Roman left his hotel, his muscles tense and his head throbbing with the beginning of a headache. It had been a long flight, and the conversation with Anna hadn't exactly been relaxing. He barely waited for his bodyguards to get in the back of his car before slamming on the gas, the tires screeching.

By the time he parked the car and headed toward Luke's penthouse, Roman was in such a foul mood even his bodyguards kept a careful distance behind him.

"Wait here," he said before using his key card and stepping into the private lift.

At last, the doors slid open and he stepped out into the empty living room.

A delicious smell was coming from the kitchen. Roman headed there, his footsteps muffled by the plush carpet.

He leaned against the kitchen doorway, feeling the tension in his muscles dissipate.

Luke was singing softly as he stood by the stove, stirring the sauce in the pot. He was wearing a pair of denim shorts and a bright Hawaiian t-shirt, his golden curls pushed back with a flowery headscarf.

A set of large headphones was perched on his curly head, Luke's hips swaying a little as he hummed some song. He looked very young, very endearing, and very ridiculous—not exactly a combination Roman normally found attractive.

He couldn't look away.

Silently, he walked over, pushed the curls aside and pressed his lips to Luke's nape.

Luke stiffened for a moment before relaxing and leaning back against Roman's chest. "You're early," he said, taking his headphones off. He tried to turn around, but Roman didn't let him, his hands gripping Luke's hips and holding him in place while he sucked bruises into his flawless skin, inhaling his sweet scent greedily and feeling his headache recede.

"How—how did it go?" Luke said. "The meeting, I mean?"

"As well as expected," Roman replied, trailing his lips up Luke's neck, to his cheek. "Canberra is satisfied with the new partner I introduced him to."

Luke leaned into the touch, his full lips parting. He seemed to be having trouble keeping his eyes open. "Did you make it clear he knows Whitford Industries won't be making deals with the likes of him any longer?"

"Yes," Roman said curtly before tugging the collar of Luke's t-shirt aside and sucking a mark into the creamy skin of his shoulder.

Luke squirmed. "Stop that," he said hoarsely with a smile. "I have to finish making dinner and I can't do it when you're all over me. Go sit over there." He pushed Roman toward the chair.

Roman did sit down, albeit reluctantly.

Leaning back in his chair, he glanced at the steamer and raised an incredulous brow. "Are you cooking *manti*?"

A pink flush colored Luke's cheeks. He shrugged nonchalantly, returning to stirring the sauce. "I guess I developed a bit of a taste for it while I was in Russia. It's not a hard dish to make. I got bored today and decided to try my hand at it." He shrugged again.

He was a terrible liar.

Roman's lips twitched.

Luke shot him a sideways look. "Shut up," he said, his right dimple making an appearance as an embarrassed smile curled his lips. He must have been aware how pathetically lovesick his behavior was.

Roman didn't comment on it. Just as he never commented on how Luke looked at him, curled into him, and gave him his lips to kiss at every opportunity.

A better man would have nipped this in the bud and told Luke to turn his affections elsewhere, to someone who was worthy of them. But even the thought of some other man touching Luke's skin, kissing his plump, sweet lips, and fucking that nice little body made Roman's hands clench into fists.

He wasn't a better man. Because no matter how pathetically obvious the boy's feelings were, Roman found himself wanting *moremoremore*, ruthlessly greedy, taking every bit of Luke's affections and unwilling to give it up.

"Penny for your thoughts?" Luke said, setting a delicious smelling plate of food in front of Roman and turning away to fill his own plate.

Roman reached out, took his wrist and pulled him into his lap.

Luke giggled. "No, let's eat first," he said. Contrary to his words, his arms looped around Roman's neck. "You know we won't get any eating done if we start. I'm hungry. You must be hungry too."

He was. He always was.

"Canberra was the last," Roman said.

It took Luke a few moments to understand what it meant. "Oh," he said, his face falling.

Fucking hell. Did the boy not understand how dangerous it was to wear one's heart on one's sleeve?

"Yes," Roman said. "Everything has been taken care off. There will be no more threats."

Luke curled his hands in his own lap. "So…Are you, like, leaving?" he said, his expression open and vulnerable.

Jesus fucking Christ. What the hell was this human being doing in Roman's lap, *looking* at him that way?

I never thought I'd see a day you'd let some baby-faced English kid plait ropes out of you.

Anna's words that Luke had him wrapped around his little finger had put him on edge—because she wasn't wrong.

Denying it was pointless. It was hard to deny it when Luke was the sole reason Roman was relocating his headquarters to a different country. He understood why Anna was so surprised: a part of him still couldn't believe he was doing it, either. And that was only one of the many compromises he would have to make.

Looking at the boy's earnest, anxious face, Roman couldn't bring himself to care.

He lifted a hand and tucked a stray curl behind Luke's ear. "How are your therapy sessions going? Any luck getting cured of me?"

Leaning into his hand like a touch-starved kitten, Luke glared at him. "Stop making fun of me."

"I'm not making fun of you," Roman said, holding his gaze. "This is a serious question."

Luke dropped his eyes for a moment before looking back at him with a humorless smile. "I think the answer is pretty obvious, yeah?" He wet his lips with his tongue. "Looks like I have a chronic, incurable form."

Trying to ignore the disgustingly warm feeling in the region of his heart, Roman cleared his throat and said, "You're an idiot."

Luke nodded, the corners of his lips turning down. His eyes suspiciously shiny, he blinked a few times before burying his face in Roman's chest. "I feel so stupid," he whispered. "I never meant for this to happen. Not with you. Even before you, I always got hung up on guys who were all wrong for me. You're, like, the worst of them all, but I never had it this bad." His voice cracked. "What the fuck is wrong with me?"

If Roman were a better man, he would assure Luke there was nothing wrong with him and that he had plenty of time to meet a good man who would deserve him.

But, as far as he was concerned, there wasn't a man good enough to lick this precious boy's boots. The world was full of selfish assholes like him. At least Roman was an asshole who could protect him and take care of him.

"You asked me if I was leaving," Roman said, burying his fingers in Luke's curls. He could never resist them. "Do you want me to stick around?"

Luke lifted his head and looked at him with a frown. "Does it matter what I want?"

There was confusion and incredulity in his tone, and Roman got the sudden urge to kill every single man who was to blame.

"You're asking the wrong question," Roman said, his voice clipped and rough as he peered into Luke's eyes. "You should be asking yourself whether you want it or not. You and I both know I'm not a nice man. A man like me has no business with someone like you. If you're smart, you'll tell me to get out of your life, Curly."

Chuckling, he brushed Luke's temple with his thumb. "Do it now while you still can. Because once you're mine, you're mine." He inhaled and exhaled slowly. "I already think of you as mine, but I think—I *think* I can still stop and leave you alone." *Maybe.* "But if you choose to be mine, that's it. Even if your perfect nice man ever shows up, you won't stop being mine." *I'll fucking kill him, and it's not an exaggeration.* "So think carefully. It's your call, not mine."

Luke's eyes were wide, full of bewilderment, disbelief, and something very bright and warm.

At last, a slow smile stretched his lips. "I would say I want to be yours," he said. "But I'm already yours."

Roman didn't know whether to laugh or curse.

"You're an idiot," he said again, cradling the boy's heart-shaped face in his hands.

"Maybe, but I don't care," Luke said, turning his face to kiss Roman's palm. "I want to be happy. You make me happy."

Fuck dinner. Dinner could wait.

"I will." Roman pressed his lips against Luke's, stood up, and carried him toward the bedroom.

He had a boy to make happy.

Chapter 29

"You look different," James said, looking at him from across the table.

Luke shrugged and dug into his salad, refusing to be self-conscious about his pink floral button down or his white skinny jeans. If anyone thought he looked flamboyant, it wasn't Luke's problem. He was done feeling embarrassed about who he was. He felt good in these clothes. That was the important thing.

"Mate…" James said cautiously. "Is that man forcing you to dress like that?"

Luke blinked. "What?"

Realizing James was actually serious, he started giggling.

He knew James hadn't exactly been thrilled when Luke had told him that he was seeing Roman, but Luke hadn't realized the extent of it. It was the first time they were hanging out in nearly a month.

"Hey, it's not funny," James said. "I'm worried, you git. First you start shagging the guy who had you kidnapped for months, now you're changing yourself for him."

"I'm not changing myself for him," Luke said with a crooked smile. "This is who I am. This is who I've always been. The only thing he changed was…he helped me see there was nothing wrong with me. I no longer feel like I have to hide it."

James's pale brows drew together, his blue-green eyes filled with confusion. "But why didn't you say anything before? Did you think I would judge you?"

Luke met his gaze. "I distinctly remember you telling me how much you disliked Fred's flamboyance and femininity."

James flushed. "I disliked Fred because he wasn't Ryan, not because…I kept comparing him to Ryan, so everything about him annoyed me—"

"I can't blame you for being attracted to hunks," Luke said, chuckling. "That would be very hypocritical of me."

They shared an amused look before James turned serious. "I really don't care, you know that, right? I'm sorry if I gave you that impression." He smirked a little. "You can wear a skirt and I will still love you, Lucy."

Rolling his eyes, Luke kicked him under the table. "I'm not into cross-dressing. I just like pretty things, and I've decided I'm not going to care if some narrow-minded people think it's strange or effeminate. Gender stereotypes are stupid, anyway. I'm happy the way I am."

"You do look happy."

Luke smiled, thinking of the past few months. "Because I am happy."

James eyed him thoughtfully. "You're serious about him, aren't you?"

Luke met his friend's eyes. "I've never been more serious."

"It's just kind of crazy," James said, sighing. "You realize that, right? He's a man who kidnapped you and forced himself onto you."

Luke frowned. "I told you already: he never forced me to do anything I didn't want. Yes, Roman is very far from being a saint, but one thing he isn't is a rapist. So drop it, okay?"

James pressed his lips together. "I just can't see it working long-term. He's going to break your heart."

Luke looked down at his hands. "Aren't all people in relationships in danger of that happening? If we live in constant fear of having our hearts broken, we'll never take the chance to be happy."

"Yeah, but that man is—"

"That man," Luke cut him off, a slight edge appearing in his voice, "is the man who makes me happier than I've ever been. Please respect it. Please."

"Sorry," James said, wincing. "You do look very happy. I just don't want you to get hurt."

"I don't want me to get hurt, either," Luke said calmly. "Look, I get where you're coming from, but I don't think you have a reason to worry. Roman—he…" Luke trailed off, thinking of going to sleep in Roman's arms and waking up so tangled with him that it was hard to tell where Roman ended and he began. Luke smiled softly. "He cares for me. I know he does."

James's expression remained skeptical. "Has he told you that? That he loves you?"

Luke gave a short laugh. "I haven't exactly said the words, either. It's just—it doesn't matter—I mean, of course it matters, but—" He cut himself off, frustrated by his inability to put his thoughts into words.

"He's not really the type to talk about feelings, and I don't think the words are all that important. I think what you feel around the person is more important than pretty words. And I feel…" Warmth spread from his chest to his face. "I feel fucking *cherished* when I'm with him. Like I'm something precious. And that means more to me than any sweet words."

"Oh," James said, his face finally softening. He smiled. "Fine, okay. If he makes you that happy, that's all that matters. But aren't you scared? Even a bit?"

Luke smiled back. "I'm scared shitless. But not for the reasons you think. I'm scared of scaring him off. You know what I've always dreamed of."

A wrinkle appeared on James's forehead. "A nice guy to build a family with. You still want it?"

"I don't want a nice guy," Luke said, snorting. "Roman kind of ruined all other men for me. I want only him." *All the time.* "But the thing is, I didn't stop wanting other things. I still want kids. I want a family of my own. But wanting them with him isn't just stupid—it's dangerous. He is who he is. I get super anxious every time I don't hear from him while he's away. Bringing kids into the picture would only make it worse even if Roman was willing to."

"Wait," James said, his eyes widening. "Kids? Don't you think it's a bit too fast? Even Ryan and I haven't discussed kids and we've been inseparable since childhood!"

"Obviously I don't want kids now," Luke said with a laugh. "To be honest, I don't think I'm anywhere near ready to share him with anyone. I want him all to myself."

Luke blushed. He'd never thought he was capable of being so possessive. It was kind of mortifying. "But you know me, Jim. At some point in the future, I would love to have his babies." Even thinking of dark-haired, blue-eyed little boys and girls made him smile dreamily. Luke sighed. "And I shouldn't want it. I'm just setting myself up for disappointment."

James looked thoughtful. "I think you should ask him. It's better to test the waters now, to see if he's open to the idea. This way, if he refuses point blank, at least you'll know for sure it's not a possibility. It'll suck, yeah, but honesty is always the best policy." James smiled without much humor. "Lying and hiding what you want for years is never a good idea, trust me."

"Don't you think it would be pushy? I don't want to be too pushy."

James snorted. "You're, like, the opposite of pushy, mate."

Luke almost laughed. James just hadn't seen him with Roman. He hadn't seen how insatiable and needy Luke was with him. Luckily for him, Roman seemed to like it, but surely there must be some boundaries? Talking about children so early in a relationship was probably one of them.

"I'll think about it," Luke said, frowning. James's advice was sound, but he couldn't imagine Roman giving the positive answer.

"Hey, chin up," James said, knocking their knees together. "I don't want your Russian mobster to come after me because I upset his boy."

Luke chuckled. "Don't be ridiculous," he said, blushing a little.

He knew Roman *would* care if he saw him upset, and that knowledge warmed him to the tips of his toes.

Maybe Roman would say no, but maybe it didn't matter.

This was enough for him. More than enough.

Chapter 30

Roman had never been the cuddling type. Sometimes he had humored his partners, but he'd never particularly enjoyed it himself. But he couldn't deny that he liked the weight of Luke's curly head on his chest, liked holding the boy close after sex, liked Luke's sleepy snuggles. He really was such a cuddle monster.

"Remember how you told me seventy percent of your business was legal?" Luke murmured suddenly.

Roman made an affirmative noise, threading his fingers through the boy's hair.

"You could make it one hundred percent."

Roman opened his eyes. "What?"

Luke folded his arms on top of Roman's chest and put his chin on them, his expression earnest but hesitant. "You're a multi-billionaire. It wouldn't make a big difference for you. It would be practically a drop in the ocean."

Roman laughed. "Not exactly a drop in the ocean."

Luke's brows furrowed. "You'd never need so much money."

"I likely wouldn't," Roman conceded.

"See?" Luke exclaimed, beaming at him, dimples in full force.

Roman suppressed a sigh. "And why, exactly, should I give up thirty percent of my income?" he said dryly. "We're talking about millions here. And before you say it's the 'right' thing to do, I never cared about doing the right thing and I'm not going to start."

"It's not—I'm not talking about doing the right thing. I mean, of course doing the right thing is important, but that's not the main reason." Luke went silent for a short while. "I know you think my father was an idiot, but he wasn't. He was smart, cunning, and dangerous. And yet he's dead."

Biting his lip, Luke dropped his gaze for a moment before meeting Roman's eyes again. "I get nervous every time you don't call me for long while you're away. I want to stop feeling that way, stop living in fear."

Roman stared at him, a warm feeling spreading through his chest, a sensation that had become very familiar as of late.

"I'm not easy to kill, *solnyshko*," he said, and for the first time he noticed there was no trace of mockery in the endearment. Perhaps there hadn't been for a while. *Solnyshko* fit. Sunshine. His little sun.

Luke gave a small smile that didn't quite touch his eyes. "I'm sure my father thought the same. Please?"

Roman was used to dealing with dangerous men. Many would call him a very dangerous man, as well. But this slim young man with his angelic face, soft smiles, golden curls and earnest eyes was the most dangerous thing he'd ever encountered. This face should have been outlawed.

Roman tightened his arm around Luke's back before flipping him over and rolling on top of him. He leaned down and kissed the plush, cherry pink lips lightly, then again, and again. His body was completely sated after the sex, but he was hungry, a hunger that had nothing to do with lust. He wanted to swallow this boy's sweetness and make it his own.

"Is that a yes?" Luke gasped against his lips.

"It's a maybe," Roman said, propping himself up on his elbows. It was a complicated issue. Of course he could find legal alternatives to partly compensate for the lost income, but rationally, there was no viable reason to change what was working perfectly. However, he had known this would likely be one of the compromises he would have to make if he wanted to keep the boy—and keep him safe.

He had already assessed the situation.

But Luke didn't need to know that. Luke didn't need to know how whipped he was. "It's not a decision I can make on a whim."

"I know," Luke said, his eyes full of light. He touched Roman's unshaven cheek. "I kind of thought you'd refuse outright. It means a lot to me that you will consider it."

Smirking, Roman murmured, "But what's in it for me? What about some shares of Whitford Industries?"

Luke half-groaned, half-laughed. "You're impossible!"

No, you're impossible, Roman thought, looking down at Luke's grinning face. *What are you doing with me, letting my tainted hands touch you?*

He didn't say it aloud. He never claimed to be a good man.

Instead, Roman rolled on his back, wondering if Luke had any idea what he'd gotten himself into. He was so young, only twenty-three. Did the boy truly realize there was no going back for him? Because Roman would never let him go.

Luke snuggled up to him again, fingers playing idly with his chest hair. "Can I ask you something?" There was something strange in his voice. "Promise not to freak out on me," he added against Roman's biceps.

Looking at his curly head, Roman chuckled. "Not exactly a promising beginning."

Luke was carefully avoiding his eyes. "Do you want to have kids at some point?"

"It's not that I'm opposed to that," Roman replied, his tone neutral as he eyed Luke. Truth be told, it was an issue he'd given some thought to after turning thirty. His mother's constant nagging for grandchildren aside, he did like the idea of leaving the fortune he had amassed to his own children. Because Luke was right about one thing: Roman wouldn't be able to spend all his money in several lifetimes. But there were other issues to consider. A child was a huge responsibility. A child would be another weak point his enemies might use against him.

"But it's probably more hassle than it's worth," Roman said. "It's not safe." Yet.

"Oh," Luke said, his eyelashes hiding his expression.

Roman stared at him. "You can't seriously want children with me."

Blushing a little, Luke met his gaze steadily. "Why not? Do you expect me to have children with some other man?"

"Don't even joke about that," Roman said, laying his hand on Luke's nape. "You're mine."

An amused but pleased smile appeared on Luke's face. "Hmm, I think it's only the third time you said that today. You might need to say it a few more times." The boy's smile turned a bit sly. "Might need to piss on me or something."

Roman gripped Luke's chin in his hand. "You think I won't?"

"Um. That's..." Luke blushed bright red and glared at Roman. "Don't derail the subject. We were talking about having babies. Like, together. At some point." He chewed on his lip. "Don't you want to? If you're, like, serious about me?"

Roman almost smiled. It wasn't the first time Luke had carefully avoided talking about feelings, as if Luke thought Roman was emotionally stunted and incapable of talking about them. It was amusing. Roman was a grown man. He was fully capable of owning up to his feelings once he had acknowledged their existence.

"But I already have a baby," Roman said, touching Luke's cheek with his thumb.

A strangled laugh left Luke's lips. "Don't be silly—I'm talking about real babies."

"Are you saying you aren't a real baby?" Roman leaned down and bit Luke's earlobe lightly. "I could have sworn you called me 'daddy' just an hour ago."

Luke slapped his chest. "Oh my God, I'm trying to have a serious conversation here!"

"Fine." Roman propped himself on an elbow and studied him intently. "You really want it? To have a home with me? Raise children together?"

Luke nodded, looking flustered but eager. "At some point."

Staring at him, Roman imagined curly-haired, dimpled toddlers running to greet him after he returned home from a long, stressful business trip. The idea wasn't unappealing. It wasn't unappealing at all.

"I can't promise that it will happen anytime soon," Roman said. "Before it can become possible, there are things to be set in motion." *And enemies to take care of.* He supposed starting a family was a respectable reason to do a big cleanup. "It might take years."

Luke gazed at him in disbelief before a bright smile split his face and he lunged forward to kiss Roman, grinning like mad and hugging him tightly. "I love you, love you, love you!" he said breathlessly between kisses. Luke froze, flushing, and laughed awkwardly. "You don't have to say it back. I just wanted you to know."

"You're an idiot," Roman said and Luke's face turned adorably confused and a little hurt. Like a kitten. A little kitten with his claws sunk right into him.

"I love you, too, you silly boy," Roman said, his voice gruff. When Luke's eyes widened, Roman's lips twisted. "I wish I didn't. They say love brings out the worst in a man. I'm almost scared of what I'm capable of if anyone tries to take you away from me." He stroked Luke's cheek with his knuckles, holding Luke's unblinking, misty-eyed gaze. "You should have told me to leave while you still could, sweetheart. I'm not a good man. Not good enough for someone like you."

Luke shook his head slowly. "You're good to me. Is it bad that's all I care about?"

Roman chuckled. "You're asking the wrong person, love."

Luke was still staring at him unblinkingly. "Don't you care I'm a guy?" he murmured, chewing on his lip. "You used to think it's unnatural to want a family with a man. People are going to talk."

Roman smoothed the furrow between Luke's brows with his thumb. "If anyone has a problem with you—with us—they're more than welcome to say it to my face."

Luke laughed. "Right. But I'm sure your family won't approve. Like, your mother. She's probably...very traditional."

Roman's lips curled. "I'm a big boy. I can live without my mother's approval. But I doubt she will care as long as I provide her with a brood of grandchildren. Besides, she's about as intimidating as a wet sponge. She's a nagging, spoiled lady with a penchant for pretty things." Smirking, he pinched Luke's cheek. "You'll get along just fine."

Luke's bottom lip poked out in a pout. "You're making fun of me," he grumbled, but his eyes were radiant with warmth and happiness. He leaned his cheek against Roman's and sighed in contentment as Roman started stroking his curls.

They fell into a comfortable silence, bodies pressed tightly against each other.

Roman knew it wasn't going to be as easy as he made it out to be. There were things to be set in motion. He was going to make quite a few people unhappy with him. But with Luke in his arms, it all seemed insignificant. Irrelevant. Easy.

Roman wondered when this soft-hearted, bright-eyed human being had become his home, his safe place.

He didn't know.

What he knew was that he would do just about anything to keep his safe place safe.

"You know what I want right now?" Luke said with a small, happy smile. "I want to have slow, sappy vanilla sex for a change."

"I think it's called making love," Roman said, nudging Luke's nose with his own.

"Yeah," Luke murmured, grinning against Roman's lips. "Let's make love."

"Let's," Roman said and kissed his sweet lips, greedy and possessive. *No one will take you away from me. No one.*

Let them try.

The End

About the Author

Alessandra Hazard is the author of the bestselling MM romance series *Straight Guys* and *Calluvia's Royalty*.

Visit Alessandra's website to learn more about her books: http://www.alessandrahazard.com/books/

To be notified when Alessandra's new books become available, you can subscribe to her mailing list: http://www.alessandrahazard.com/subscribe/

You can contact the author at her website or email her at author@alessandrahazard.com.

72343630R00154

Made in the
USA
Middletown, DE